It was nearly dark. Hubert stood for a moment with his eyes on Tabbie's face, only conscious of her nearness and the hand on his arm. It was very quiet, in fact almost breathlessly still, and into the silence the bird's song suddenly broke in a silvery cadence of sound. To have Tabbie as close as this, with her smiling face turned towards him, her hand touching him, was almost more than he could stand.

He said abruptly, "I think we had better join the others, Tabbie, because if we don't, with that moon swinging up over those trees and that damned bird breaking my heart, I shall make love to you. And that would not be at all the thing."

The words were sharply, almost roughly spoken, the tone of his voice harsh and ironical, daring her to believe him, inviting her to laugh at him with himself, and then he turned and walked away towards the house, leaving her to follow, near to laughter and yet even nearer to tears.

That night she did not sleep very well. . . .

THE
GLASS PALACE

Mary Ann Gibbs

A FAWCETT CREST BOOK

Fawcett Publications, Inc., Greenwich, Connecticut

THE GLASS PALACE

THIS BOOK CONTAINS THE COMPLETE TEXT OF
THE ORIGINAL HARDCOVER EDITION.

A Fawcett Crest Book reprinted by arrangement with Mason/
Charter Publishers, Inc.

ISBN   0-449-23063-5

Printed in the United States of America

10   9   8   7   6   5   4   3   2   1

CHAPTER

1

The hall was very quiet: at any moment now the dressing-bell would sound and Aunt Aggie and Louisa would come out of the drawing-room and go upstairs to dress, pausing on the way to have a few words with her, smiling, lightly pitying.

"Poor Tabbie!" they would say. "Still waiting? Where is that naughty Arnold tonight?" And they would go on up the stairs.

After that the smoking-room door would open and her Uncle Joseph would emerge, possibly with Major Rawlings, heavily humorous about Arnold's tardiness.

Tabitha Sackroyd, in her bonnet and shawl, sat down reluctantly to wait, wishing she could take refuge in the morning-room—only the fire there was out—or in her bedroom, only that would give the servants unnecessary trouble as they would have to fetch her when Arnold arrived, which would arouse her aunt's disapproval. Servants, she told her niece, were trouble enough, without having them sulk because they had to run all over the house after her.

The shadows of the flunkeys in the lobby moved against the glass doors that separated it from the entrance hall as they talked and laughed together. She wondered what they were laughing at, secure behind those doors in a world of their own. Here on this side all was as quiet as the grave.

The new gas chandelier suspended from the high ceiling cast a pool of light immediately below it, dwelling on the orange palm leaves and deep red background of the Kidderminster carpet. Beyond that circle the colours were almost lost, swallowed by the shadows of the heavy carved furniture, until they were picked up by the firelight and given a more subdued glow.

The house, one of a row of mansions that had been built on the site of the old hot-houses and pineries of Kensington Palace and renamed Palace Gardens, was referred to by Sir Joseph Sackroyd as his "town house," while the large new red-brick villa near the small country town of Westways was "my country place in Surrey." A very rich man was Sir Joseph with a fortune derived from trade, and he liked to think that his houses and family were fitted to his position in the world.

Tabbie had got engaged to Arnold Jarrett when the family was at Westways for the summer five years ago: he had been the new curate there, under a Rector who wintered abroad on account of his wife's health, taking his family with him. Living alone in lodgings near one of the public houses in the town, Arnold had been glad to escape to the family of young people at The Grange, and his welcome had increased in warmth when Sir Joseph and his lady realised that he was seriously attracted to their orphaned niece. It was very convenient to have Tabbie safely engaged to a young man in the Church, a future as a clergyman's wife being in Sir Joseph's eyes the most suitable for her. He had every hope that Arnold Jarrett would speedily follow the example of his predecessor, young Cray, who had been given a first-rate living in the North of England only a year after he came to Westways. Granted he had married the Rector's eldest daughter, which might have made a difference, but Sir Joseph would not admit that his niece was a worse bargain than the Rector's Maria.

But after their return to Kensington it appeared that the only situation Arnold could obtain was another curacy, this time in Kensington, and while it was better than the Westways curacy because he was able to live with his mother and could see Tabbie nearly every day, it did not seem that his prospects of getting a living had improved.

Sir Joseph had begun to make enquiries among his friends to discover if any of them had livings to dispose of, and he had no doubt that if the young man had not fallen into the unhappy way of attacking his prospective benefactors in his sermons, he might have been successful.

"What does he know about the sin of riches on his stipend?" he asked his eldest son Augustus one Sunday evening over a game of chess, after a particularly virulent attack by Arnold in church that morning during the Vicar's absence with a cold. "He would find it nothing to laugh at if he were a rich man, being bullied and begged at every hour of the day, and by a lot of humbugs into the bargain."

"I thought that Arnold had prospects on his mother's side?" Augustus, married and comfortably settled in

Queen's Square, Bloomsbury, had his father's shrewd eye
for business. "Is there not an uncle, a well-to-do bachelor
with only Arnold to inherit his money?"

"There was such an uncle when I permitted Tabbie to
get engaged to Arnold," said Sir Joseph resentfully. "That
is what made me think it would be a good match for her,
with no money of her own beyond five hundred pounds in
the funds. She has been utterly dependent on myself since
she was born, but being my only sister's child naturally
we adopted her on her mother's death and I have tried to
do my best for her." His voice rose peevishly. "I do not
think anyone could say that I should have done more."

Augustus wondered why his father always defended his
behaviour to Tabbie in this way: surely the benevolence
he had shown was something to be proud of and nobody
could condemn him for it? While he thought about it Sir
Joseph went on: "If only Arnold would preach the comfortable sermons we were accustomed to hearing from
young Cray down in Westways I am sure I could find him
a living in no time."

"I hear," said Augustus, "that young Cray now keeps
his carriage and pair."

"I am not surprised. I should have been surprised if he
did not. That young man had very good manners, and
drank his port as if he enjoyed it and not as if it were a
brand of poison. I am extremely disappointed in Arnold."

His disappointment made itself felt in the coolness of
his manner towards the young man and in the slighting
tone in which he asked after his uncle—who had most
disobligingly married a young girl soon after Arnold got
engaged to Tabbie and had produced a young family of
his own. These enquiries and coolness brought a flush to

his niece's cheek and a feeling in her swelling heart that poor Arnold was being very hard done by.

And now pretty Louisa was engaged to Major Harry Rawlings of the 13th Light Dragoon Guards, the only son of the Hon. Baveystoke Rawlings of Perle Place in Hampshire, and the wedding was to be in June, while her own wedding to Arnold was as far away as ever.

The clock ticked on in its corner as she moved impatiently, wondering where he could have got to tonight, and if—with a further depression of spirits—he was with Miss Fulgrove.

At the beginning of the summer, soon after the family had departed to Westways, Selina Fulgrove had become the tenant of a house in Addison Road. She was a wealthy woman, dark-haired and handsome, accustomed to having her own way and addicted to a rather ostentatious form of benevolence. She brought with her a Mrs. Gaywood to act as chaperone, who played her part with a good-natured cheerfulness and was an old enough friend not to hesitate to speak her mind if the necessity for it arose. Selina was fond of her and respected her judgement—if only second to her own.

In Tabbie's absence Arnold had immediately succumbed to the fascination of Miss Fulgrove's wealth, looks and philanthropy, and it was easy to respond to her demands on his time and interest as Mrs. Jarrett's house was in Edwardes Square, tucked away behind Earl's Terrace and scarcely a stone's throw from Addison Road.

When Tabbie returned he tried to explain that the needs of the poor in the parish were endless and there were few people so eager to alleviate them as the charming Miss Fulgrove, and he lost no time in introducing his betrothed to the lady. Tabbie thought it must be something contrary in her own nature that made her dislike the paragon on sight and her dislike did not lessen as she got to know her better. For one thing she soon discovered that excellent as Miss Fulgrove was at starting soup kitchens and clothing clubs and penny readings for the destitute poor, her enthusiasm for such projects seldom lasted beyond the first fortnight, and then they would be thankfully handed over to Miss Capp and Miss Knagg, two worthy ladies, neighbours of the Jarretts, who taught in the Sunday school and were district visitors besides.

No, Tabbie did not like Miss Fulgrove.

The dressing-bell sounded deafeningly and the ladies emerged from the drawing-room.

"Dear me, Tabbie, Arnold *is* late tonight!" said her aunt as if he had always fetched her before the dressing-bell sounded on Wednesday evenings. "Don't wait out there like a governess waiting to be interviewed, dear! The morning-room fire is out but you may go into the smoking-room. Your uncle has already gone upstairs and Harry is not here tonight—some tiresome regimental dinner I believe—so that there will be nobody there but William. You may tell him to go up and dress, if you please: otherwise he will still be poring over those wretched drains and smoking those horrid cheroots for the next half-hour or so, and I dislike him coming to dinner smelling of tobacco. Besides, he will be late and the soup will be cold."

"Yes, Aunt." Tabbie got up and made her way to the smoking-room with relief. William, the Sackroyds' second son, was more like a brother than a cousin. He had a passionate interest in drains, a subject that had fascinated him from the time he was at Cambridge and still held him enthralled. Tabbie alone had never dismissed his interest in such things as eccentricity but understood that it could be important to the health of the nation, and ever since he had written a treatise on "The Drainage Systems of our Cities," for a scientific journal, it seemed that others recognised its importance too, and quite well-known people, like Cabinet Ministers, sometimes wrote to ask his opinion on sewerage problems.

Having made this modest mark he was beginning to earn the respect of his family—if not their understanding—when his godmother in Norfolk died and it was found that she had left him her house and a few hundred acres not far from Norwich. The inheritance was not a vast one, but he set off at once to West Bassett to see it for himself and was immediately and happily aware that the task of bringing the antiquated drainage system of the pleasant country house up to date would keep him occupied for months.

For some time therefore his family saw little of him as he only visited London when his advice was needed urgently elsewhere, and on these occasions although he tried to explain to his father and Augustus what he was doing at West Bassett, in the end it was only Tabbie who showed a proper understanding of what he was talking about.

"When Arnold gets his living I shall insist on your coming to examine the drains of our vicarage," she told him soon after Louisa was engaged. "And I have told Louisa that she should persuade Harry to tell his father to ask you to look at the drains at Perle Place. As the house goes back to Tudor times they may be of that date too and far from healthy."

William had looked up from some plans in front of him then to say warmly, "I shall dance at Louisa's wedding far more happily that I shall at yours, Tabbie. You are the only person who knows what I'm at. Papa and Augustus look at my diagrams as if they were some kind of Chinese puzzle with the directions written in Greek."

Dear William. Tabbie opened the smoking-room door and then stopped short on seeing through the blue haze of tobacco smoke that he had a visitor with him, a tall, broad-shouldered man of about thirty-five years of age.

Hubert Ashley was a physician who had moved from London to a pleasant house in Old Brompton the year before, and such was his popularity that many of his London patients came to consult him still, their carriages standing in his drive for hours at a time.

The only son of a rich man, he had embarked on a successful army career when the girl he was engaged to marry developed consumption and died a month before the wedding-day at the early age of seventeen. The agony of watching her die had made him determine to ease the lot of others in similar situations, and he had sold his commission and gone to St. Bartholomew's Hospital to study medicine. He had showed so great an aptitude for the profession and so great an understanding of the human problems that were bound up in it that he had eventually become one of the best known physicians in the country. He had never married and his remaining unmarried sister, Blanche, kept house for him, but as she had an excellent housekeeper, Mrs. Webb by name, she did not find these duties onerous, and had recently consented to become lady superintendent of St. Ursula's, a small hospital for sick ladies that had recently been opened in Old Brompton. Brother and sister went their ways with great cheerfulness and good humour, meeting at meal-times with subjects of mutual interest to discuss.

The doctor was standing by a table where William was poring over some plans that his visitor had brought for him to examine. Both men were smoking cheroots with enjoyment and neither heard the opening of the door.

"I beg your pardon, William," Tabbie said, glancing a little uncertainly from the doctor to the back of William's head with its thatch of unruly hair. "Aunt Aggie wished me to remind you that the dressing-bell had gone."

"Bless you, Tabbie, I heard it. That new footman of Mamma's makes enough noise to wake the dead." William turned in his chair to smile at her, his pleasant face with its rather heavy features expressing nothing but interest in the papers that absorbed him. And then suddenly he remembered his manners and put down his cheroot to say, "But here is Dr. Ashley. You know him, don't you?"

"How do you do, Dr. Ashley?" Tabbie acknowledged him gravely. "The last time we met I was hoarse as a crow and you prescribed some excellent medicine."

"Did you take it, or did you pour it away?" he asked, putting down his cheroot as well, and was instantly rewarded by her laugh as she flashed a mischievous glance at him.

"I took a great deal of it," she protested. "At least six spoonsful and it was very nasty."

"There should have been twenty-four doses in the bottle if the chemist made it up correctly."

"But I was quite recovered." She came over to the table and looked at the plans laid out there. "Are those the plans to your house, Dr. Ashley? Because before you hand them over to William you should be careful that you know what you are about. In almost no time at all your ground floor will be open to the cellars."

He studied her with respect tempered with surprise.

This girl, in spite of her sober dress, was alive and charming, far removed from the shadowy little creature he had seen for a few minutes in her aunt's morning-room. Then there had not been time to do more than glance at a reddened throat and promise to send his page-boy round with medicine, because Lady Sackroyd had been impatient to be rid of him. Her housekeeper wanted to see her about a dinner-party she was giving that night and she was irritated at being delayed by so unimportant a matter as her niece's sore throat, and in fact her manner had implied that it had been invented just to annoy her.

"Fortunately, Miss Sackroyd, these plans are nothing to do with me," he told her. "They belong to St. Ursula's, and having heard from Sir Joseph that Mr. William was expected this week my sister asked me to bring a problem for him to solve for her. She is worried about one corner of a small ward where there is a smell. No patient in that corner ever prospers, in fact she tends to sicken until she is removed from it. At first Blanche thought it might be due to contagion but now she thinks there may be poisonous fumes from a nearby drain, a view that your cousin here endorses."

"I have been telling Dr. Ashley about our Cousin Mary's drawing-room in Marling down in Berkshire," William said. "You remember the smell there was in that room, Tabbie?"

"Nobody could forget it." Tabbie wrinkled her nose. "Dr. Ashley, it was a terrible smell. Our cousin insisted on having the windows set wide open when that room was used: she said it was better to catch cold from sitting in a gale of wind than retiring to bed with bad throats."

"I persuaded her to have the drawing-room floor up,

nonetheless," William said. "And as I suspected, there was a crack down the main drainage pipe that passed directly under the room."

"In a private house it may be a simple matter to locate a bad smell," said the doctor. "But in a hospital it is often difficult to distinguish one smell from another, as the whole place reeks. St. Ursula's is in that respect more like a private house—indeed, as you know, it was a private house until recently. My sister too is fortunate in having a head nurse who has her floors scrubbed and her windows open, but in that particular ward a very drainlike odour still persists." He collected the papers together and thanked William for his help. "I will tell Blanche what you say, and advise her to have the workmen in to take up that floor."

"And I must obey the dressing-bell." They went out into the hall and found Arnold there in his waterproof overcoat, put out and annoyed because Tabbie was not there waiting for him "like a governess waiting to be interviewed."

When Hubert Ashley understood that he had called in order to walk with Miss Sackroyd to Edwardes Square at the far end of the High Street, he immediately offered the use of the carriage that was standing at the door.

"No, I insist," he said, standing there on the pavement beside the open carriage door. "It is a raw February night and it is drizzling with rain—or sleet—and I am sure Miss Sackroyd has only thin slippers on her feet. I know what my sister wears when she goes out of an evening: the soles of her shoes are like paper."

"On the contrary, Dr. Ashley, I am wearing boots of a stoutness quite suitable to the evening." Tabbie had seen the clouds gathering on Arnold's brow: he disliked Dr.

Ashley and would never give a reason for that dislike, though Tabbie sometimes suspected it was because the doctor was too successful for his liking. Her protest was however brushed aside.

"It will be much more comfortable for you to ride," the doctor said. "I will mount the box and take the reins and get the smell of tobacco out of my hair. My sister objects strongly to the smell of tobacco, and we are going to a musical evening tonight. There will be more room for you and Mr. Jarrett in the carriage without me, and you will come to no harm, I promise you. I am a good driver."

Tabbie did not protest any further. She got into the carriage thankfully and Arnold followed her, still very annoyed. The groom shut the door on them and followed his master up on to the box: it was a fine carriage, the upholstery of the best cord, the heavy tassels looking as if they had come only that day from the coach-builders.

"Well, isn't this nice?" Tabbie was pleased at the thought of arriving at Mrs. Jarrett's house without mud on her footwear and her petticoats. "Wasn't it kind of Dr. Ashley?"

"I do not think so." Arnold was deeply offended. "In fact I consider it to be a piece of impertinence. I detest being patronised by such people, however much others may run after them, and if I had thought a cab to be necessary for the distance from your uncle's house to my mother's, I would have hired one. I am not a pauper and I do not like to be treated as one."

Tabbie abandoned the doctor and turned her attention to more welcome subjects for conversation.

"How did the penny reading go?" she asked. "Was Miss Fulgrove there?"

"No." Arnold added hastily that another engagement had prevented her from coming. "I understand from Mrs. Gaywood that there is a young pianist that Miss Fulgrove wishes to encourage, and she has arranged a musical evening at her house for him tonight. But with the help of Miss Capp and Miss Knagg I managed the reading myself, as she knew I would of course."

"Of course." Tabbie wondered all the same if the lady's absence had not been partly the cause of Arnold's bad temper. He was full of enthusiasm for Miss Fulgrove's kindness, however, in providing cocoa and buns to be given out at the penny reading—through the auspices of Miss Capp and Miss Knagg—and Tabbie could not help feeling that under such conditions it might not be difficult to be benevolent.

He had not ceased talking about Miss Fulgrove and her kindness by the time the carriage stopped in front of Mrs. Jarrett's house and the doctor handed over the reins to his man and jumped down himself to hand the occupants out. There was a mumble of grudging thanks from Arnold as he followed his betrothed and a radiant smile from Tabbie as she let her hand rest for a moment in the doctor's.

"Thank you so much, Dr. Ashley," she said. "It was very kind of you." Her eyes went to the rain that glistened on his coat and hat and hair. "I hope you have not got very wet?"

He assured her that the rain had not wet him at all, his eyes travelling from her to Jarrett with a flicker of curiosity. In her plain bonnet and grey shawl she looked like a little Quakeress, but he thought if he had been her betrothed he would have kissed a little colour into her cheeks during the drive from her uncle's house. The man was a stick.

He remounted the box and drove on, wondering what was the secret of Tabitha Sackroyd's parentage. That she was the child of Sir Joseph's sister Tabitha nobody appeared to doubt, but at the same time few believed the story of her father, said to have been lost at sea. That was a tale too often employed for a father who disappeared long before a child was born, although Tabbie's story differed from most in that her father was supposed to have left his wife and child while on a holiday in Cornwall to go fishing in a rowing boat that had over-turned drowning him almost before his wife's eyes. Dr. Ashley, in common with several others, did not believe a word of it.

The only thing he was at all certain of was that there had been a tragedy and that Sir Joseph's sister had been the centre of it, but this evening he was suddenly convinced that her lover had been from a class as far above the Sackroyds as a swan is above farmyard geese.

The way Tabbie put out her hand, the dignified little manner in which she had recognised him in the smoking-room, the easy note in her voice as she teased William about his drains, all indicated a breeding above that of her uncle and aunt—wealthy, vulgar, purse-proud as they were.

He wished they could have found a better husband for their niece than the insufferable Jarrett, but he supposed that with her mother's history never very far from their thoughts they felt that any husband would be better than none.

CHAPTER
2

As the doctor's carriage disappeared into the drizzle of the evening Tabbie followed Arnold into the narrow hallway, where one lamp, smelling of whale oil, burned sulkily on its bracket.

"In spite of your protests," she said gaily, "I know you must have been tired and glad of the ride yourself."

"I was not tired," he replied ungraciously. "And I would have preferred to walk."

"I enjoy our walks myself," she agreed, afraid that she had hurt him. "I like hearing about the problems of the parish as we walk along together." In such a small way she could be useful to him, if not on the same scale as Miss Fulgrove. "How is Mrs. Trout?" she went on, as he took her bonnet and shawl and hung them on the row of pegs under the stairs. "I hope her ..." Here she hesitated, feeling that it might be indelicate to mention Mrs. Trout's legs, and went on quickly, "I hope she is better? I told Aunt Aggie about her and she thought it was gin. Does Mrs. Trout drink much gin, Arnold?"

"When you are as poor as Mrs. Trout," he said coldly, "a penn'orth of gin may be the only comfort left to you. Your aunt need not censure a poor old woman on that account."

"Oh, but she was not censuring her. How could she, when she does not even know her?"

"Exactly," said Arnold with a note of triumph in his voice. "Unfortunately few ladies in your aunt's position understand what it is to be poor." And then the drawing-room door on the right of the hall opened and Mrs. Jarrett came out to welcome Tabbie into the little room with its brightly burning fire.

"I heard your uncle's carriage," she said, kissing her. "I am glad he sent you in it for once."

"Oh, but he didn't." Tabbie explained about Dr. Ashley's offer to drive them and Mrs. Jarrett looked disappointed. She knew that Sir Joseph did not think it necessary to have his coachman out in the evening to drive his niece such a short distance, although he would have thought nothing of having him out to take his wife and daughter to a ball at Adelaide's house in Bayswater, and he would have expected him to stay up all night before fetching them home. But she would have liked to see his carriage outside her own door more often all the same. "Dr. Ashley drove us himself," Tabbie added smiling. "He is going to a musical evening with his sister and he wished to get the smell of tobacco out of his hair. He and William had filled the smoking-room with clouds of smoke between them."

"I daresay the Ashleys are going to Miss Fulgrove's," said Mrs. Jarrett. "Blanche Ashley has been running after

Miss Fulgrove lately: I daresay she is trying to catch her for her brother, but I don't think she will succeed. Miss Fulgrove will soon see through that little game."

Tabbie said gently that as Miss Ashley visited St. Ursula's every day she did not think she would have much time for running after anybody.

"Yes, we all know she is the lady superintendent there," said Mrs. Jarrett disagreeably. "I do not approve of ladies taking on such work—it shows a morbid mind in my opinion, to have such an interest in sick people. If she wishes to help St. Ursula's she had far better work for the bazaar we are having in July. But no, she must be different. I do not in the least see the need for her to visit the hospital every day."

Arnold remarked that as long as Dr. Ashley did not visit Miss Fulgrove too frequently it did not matter what his sister did, and added that he was not a type of man that he admired. It was obvious that he was not to be got out of his sulks.

Tabbie was relieved when Mrs. Jarrett changed the subject by admiring the dress that had been under the grey shawl, a wine-coloured velvet with muslin collar and cuffs.

"Is it a new one, Tabbie?" she asked.

"No," said Tabbie composedly. "It is an old one of Adelaide's. Isn't the velvet a lovely one? I'm fond of wine-colour for winter days."

"I am glad I have never had to wear cast-off clothing," said Mrs. Jarrett, losing her interest in the dress and trying to find worn parts in the seams unsuccessfully.

"And I, on the contrary, am very grateful for Addy's cast-offs," said Tabbie laughing. "She has excellent taste and her beautiful dresses are scarcely worn at all."

Adelaide, next to Augustus in age, had married well, and she had always treated her cousin with a kindly patronage that Tabbie had not resented, because Adelaide was kind at heart. There had been a time before she married when Tabbie had not been so happy about inheriting her dresses. Addy was taller than she was and the dresses could easily be adapted to her more slender cousin, but she had been sensitive about wearing them when they went to parties together and on more than one occasion heard their friends remarking that Tabbie was wearing Addy's dress.

But now her old dresses became welcome additions to her wardrobe, because she loved rich colours, and Lady Sackroyd selected greys and lavenders and black as being more suitable for a girl who was to become a clergyman's wife.

Mrs. Jarrett, having lost interest in her dress, started a long story about the savage cat next door and how it had attacked her poor Stripey that morning and she was only able to rescue him in the nick of time when the cat's meat man came down the street, and the horrible creature ran off after the man and his barrow. Tabbie studied Stripey thoughtfully: he was an over-fed spoiled animal and she thought that a fight might do him more good than the cat's meat man. And then the little maid brought the soup upstairs and they went into the dining-room and started supper.

Arnold remained silent during the meal and when a parishioner called to see him afterwards, leaving her alone with his mother in the drawing-room, Tabbie was encouraged to put into words a thought that had been troubling her ever since they had come back from Westways the previous autumn. She asked her future mother-in-law if she thought that Arnold ever felt he had made a mistake.

"A mistake, my dear?" Mrs. Jarrett stopped her complaints about the butcher's boy, who had thrown stones at Stripey, and looked surprised. "What can you mean? A mistake over what?"

"Over becoming engaged to me," Tabbie said simply.

"Oh, but I'm sure—I mean, I cannot think—I hope Sir Joseph and Lady Sackroyd do not think anything of the sort?" Mrs. Jarrett broke off, flustered. "Whatever made you think such a thing, my dear?"

Tabbie hesitated. If she said that he seemed to admire Miss Fulgrove so much more than herself it would sound as if she were jealous, but if on the other hand she said that he had been so cool in his manner towards her it would sound as if she were accusing him of neglect. It was all very difficult. "I just thought he might be," she said with a small stifled sigh. "It has been such a long engagement."

"He never anticipated that it would be such a long one and neither did I." Mrs. Jarrett spoke with asperity, as if it was entirely Tabbie's fault. "As you know I always said that when Arnold married I would give up this house and go to live with my sister Ada, in Leamington Spa. She has always wished me to join her there—such a nice, select place. When Arnold became engaged to you I almost wrote to tell Ada to expect me by the next train, but I did not realise—and neither did poor Arnold—that your uncle would not offer to do anything for you."

"I beg your pardon?" Tabbie frowned. "I am afraid I don't quite understand."

"It is no good putting on that air with me, my dear." Mrs. Jarrett tossed her head, her lips pursed, the ribbons in her cap quivering. She was a short, tubby woman, with iron-grey hair under the cap and a pair of small, sharp black eyes that missed nothing of what was going on about her. "Your uncle is a very rich man, and always seemed to treat you as a daughter and not merely as a poor relation, which so many men in his position might have done under the circumstances. He settled ten thousand pounds on Adelaide when she married, I believe, and I daresay he will settle twice or three times that amount on Louisa in June, as she is marrying into the aristocracy and there will be settlements to be arranged and so forth. It is quite extraordinary how grasping the aristocracy can be over matters of that sort. But it seemed to us only natural that he should do something handsome for you, and his cordial manner to Arnold encouraged him to think so. But when the dear boy asked Sir Joseph's permission to speak to you he was told that you would have your mother's money—amounting to five hundred pounds in the funds—and he appeared to think that he should be well satisfied with it. And being without any mercenary thoughts as far as you were concerned, and with my poor misguided brother being at that time unattached, he told Sir Joseph that he was perfectly content. But I must say some of our friends have thought it shabby treatment and have not hesitated to say so, especially since that dreadful young woman persuaded my brother into marrying her, and of course poor Arnold's expectations in that quarter are gone for ever."

"I am sorry if you have been disappointed in my uncle." Tabbie shrank from further discussion, but felt that she must defend the absent Sir Joseph. "I wish Arnold had told me."

"He is far too much of a Christian to mention such a

thing, my dear. Forbearance is one of his many virtues. Miss Fulgrove was saying only the other day that she wished there were more men like him. 'Sometimes, Mrs. Jarrett,' she said, 'I think your son is a saint.' "

But saints who sulked could be uncomfortable to live with perhaps and as Tabbie pondered on this Mrs. Jarrett, with a swift change of subject, turned the conversation to herself.

"Miss Fulgrove was asking about your father when she called. She brought a beautifully worked pin-cushion for the St. Ursula's bazaar. I said that I knew there had been some tragedy about his death, but I knew very little about it. He was drowned, was he not?"

"Why yes. He and my mother were making a little tour of Cornwall before he joined his ship—he was an officer in the Royal Navy—and one evening as it was a beautiful calm sea, he went fishing, leaving her alone with me in their lodgings. I was only a few months old at the time. That part of the coast is very treacherous though, and a squall blew up and the boat over-turned and he was drowned."

"A shocking thing." But Mrs. Jarrett looked more thoughtful than shocked.

"It was too much for my mother, and she died soon after, leaving me in the care of my uncle, who adopted me as his daughter and gave me his name."

"Which was your mother's name. She was a Sackroyd, was she not?"

"Of course." She was puzzled by all this interest in her history. "My father's name was Smith—Richard Algernon Smith. The initials R.A.S. are on a locker that my mother left me: it has a lock of very fair hair inside."

"Do you ever see any of his family?"

"Oh no. He was an only child and his parents were dead."

"But he must have had uncles and aunts and cousins surely? Do you not see any of them from time to time?"

"No. They live in the North I believe, and I have never known anything about them."

And then Arnold came back with the news that Mrs. Trout was so much worse that it had been thought necessary to remove her to hospital, and he was arranging for a cab to fetch her in the morning. "I will walk home with you first, though, Tabbie," he added.

Tabbie fetched her bonnet and shawl and hurried away with him. The rain had increased but no cab was summoned for her because Arnold had his umbrella. After they had gone Mrs. Jarrett folded back her skirt over her petticoat, put her feet on the fender in front of the fire, and thought over what Miss Fulgrove had said to her when she had called.

She had begun by saying that she was very sorry for Tabbie Sackroyd. "Any girl in her position is in my opinion deserving of pity," she added.

"You mean because she is only the adopted daughter of Sir Joseph and Lady Sackroyd and not their real child?" said Mrs. Jarrett, puzzled.

"Oh no. She was very lucky to be adopted by those good kind people." Selina's smile held infinite meaning. "My dear Mrs. Jarrett, you cannot surely be unaware of what is said about her? It is common gossip that the story of the father who was drowned when fishing off the Cornish coast was simply an easy way of disposing of a husband who had never existed. I had not been in Kensington for a week before I was told about it."

To Mrs. Jarrett, usually so well versed in local gossip, the information came like a thunderclap, and while it might be natural that Arnold would be left ignorant of what was generally believed about his betrothed's mother, she could not understand why she, usually so sharp in such matters, had not suspected it from the beginning.

"You think that Tabbie is the illegitimate child of Sir Joseph's sister?" she said slowly.

"That is what I believe, in common with the rest of the Sackroyds' friends. Mind you I would not like this to reach Sir Joseph's ears, but everything points to it. If her mother *had* been married to this mysterious Naval officer, would his relatives not visit Tabitha Sackroyd and would she not visit them? But one hears nothing of them: it is as if they had all gone down with him in the rowing boat!"

"That may be true, but you and I know, Miss Fulgrove, how malicious minds will exaggerate." Mrs. Jarrett was worried on her son's account. "When Arnold became engaged to Tabbie the Rector of Westways himself said that he could not have chosen a nicer girl."

"The Rector of Westways knew which side his bread was buttered," Miss Fulgrove returned cryptically. "It would not have done for him to offend Sir Joseph. And Tabitha Sackroyd *is* a nice girl: nobody could say otherwise. She is also very lucky to have become engaged to your son. I will say no more, but as you know I admire Mr. Jarrett very much and I must speak out if I think an injustice has been done. The Sackroyds knew that their niece's marriage to your son would give her the respectability that her birth lacked, and that was why Sir Joseph welcomed it. Everyone says so."

Respectability was a damning word, and yet one that

was essential in a clergyman's wife. Left alone to digest
Miss Fulgrove's information Mrs. Jarrett had thought it
over carefully.

Supposing in years to come any hint of such a scandal
touched Arnold through his wife? And if according to
their new friend everyone knew about it, where would he
be able to escape it? It was a risk that Arnold's mother
felt he should not have been allowed to take, and she
wondered hopefully if Tabbie's enquiry about Arnold's
feelings that evening had not been inspired by some impatience with their prolonged engagement on her own part.
She might be tired of it herself, and though it would be
quite scandalous for an engagement of so long a standing
to be summarily broken, it might not be a bad thing in
the end.

Tabbie had always treated Arnold in a laughing manner that held little respect, but to a lady like Miss Fulgrove, rich, handsome and well-versed in the ways of the
world, he was evidently an object of some attention. If his
engagement to Tabbie were to be at an end, he might be
encouraged to look elsewhere for a wife, and he might not
have far to go to find her.

Unaware that Miss Fulgrove spoke of Arnold to her
friend Mrs. Gaywood as "that poor little Jarrett," Mrs.
Jarrett toasted her toes on her fender and dreamed of a
time when her son might be the wealthy rector of a country parish—like the Rector of Westways—and able to go
abroad every winter with his wife, leaving the parish duties to a curate.

Over breakfast the next morning she told him what
Miss Fulgrove had said. She did not think that his affections were rooted very deeply where Tabbie was con-

cerned and she was satisfied when she found him to be as angry as she was to think that he had been used as a cat's-paw by Sir Joseph.

As they set out together for Miss Fulgrove's musical evening with the smell of tobacco gone from Dr. Ashley's hair, Hubert remarked to his sister that he had been surprised that Sir Joseph had not offered one of his carriages to his niece that evening. "It is horrible weather," he said. "Much too cold and raw for a young lady to be out walking."

"Sir Joseph is one of those people who can be generous over big things and mean over small ones," said Blanche. "He will send a footman six miles to save the expense of a postage stamp. But he appears to be fond of his niece in his pompous way, although she is the one member of the family who is naturally expected to do things to entertain the rest and save them trouble. It is she who plays chess with her uncle when his sons are not there, and if Lady Sackroyd gets her netting in a tangle she will be required to disentangle it, and if help is required at a sewing party she will be sent there—or anywhere else where nobody feels inclined to go."

"I wonder who her father was?" the doctor said.

"Everyone would like to know that, my dear."

"I daresay, but it would be interesting to know the truth of it all the same."

"There is one person who does know and that is Sir Joseph. *I* shall not ask him and I would not advise you to do so either."

"God forbid!" Hubert laughed. "I do not intend to lose

one of my wealthy patients in order to satisfy my idle curiosity."

But his thoughts continued to dwell pleasantly on Sir Joseph's niece, and during the performance of Miss Fulgrove's dull protégé on the pianoforte in her large and tasteless drawing-room, he kept seeing a pair of dark eyes raised to his with a charming serenity, and he heard the soft note in Tabitha Sackroyd's voice as she said goodbye and thanked him for the use of his carriage.

It was a long time since his interest—seldom aroused by a woman—had been so pleasantly stirred.

CHAPTER

3

There were occasions when Tabbie's presence was not required at her aunt's dinner-parties, and although they were stiff, formal affairs, given for the benefit of Sir Joseph's City friends and their wives, she was sorry to miss the music in the drawing-room afterwards. She always enjoyed music, as long as she was not asked to perform, but she was quite resigned when her aunt said at breakfast, "You won't mind, will you, my dear, if you have your dinner in the school-room tonight? Our numbers will be even without you."

Tabbie would then have her dinner by the school-room fire and curl up comfortably afterwards in the shabby arm-chair that had been the governess's, and read, trying not to listen for the sound of Louisa's singing downstairs.

When William was staying in Palace Gardens however she was required every evening to even the numbers, and Eva, the maid she shared with Louisa, came to her first to help her to dress. It was a polite fiction between them that

Tabbie had as many dresses as her cousin to choose from, whereas they both knew that apart from Adelaide's cast-off day dresses she had only three suitable for evening wear—a grey silk, a black silk, and lilac muslin. And February was scarcely a suitable month for muslins.

On the last evening of William's visit before he returned to Norfolk his mother was giving a large dinner-party and Eva lost no time in dressing Tabbie before going to Louisa.

She unhooked her brown stuff dress quickly and brushed out her hair, knotting it again with deft fingers into a shining chestnut coil on the nape of her neck. Then she removed her wrapper and slipped the grey silk over her head, hooking it over an embroidered cambric petticoat. The dress gleamed in the candlelight and the flickering flames of the fire, but Tabbie scarcely glanced at it: the young face that looked back at the maid from the mirror on her dressing-table was serious and calm and old for its years.

A wish that she had something prettier to dress her in made Eva pause a moment to give a word of encouragement. "That looks very nice, Miss," she said. The bodice of the dress was plain, the neck lace-edged, the sleeves to the elbow and lined with lace, but much as the maid twitched and pulled it, it remained in its severe simplicity more suitable for someone twice its wearer's age. Rather impatiently she took out Tabbie's jewellery—a necklace of fine coral twisted into a string, a cameo brooch, a plain gold bracelet, and her engagement ring, an opal set in pearls. A lace fan given her by her aunt the Christmas after she became engaged, and a pair of white gloves completed her dress and she was free to run off to the drawing-room, leaving Eva for Louisa whose evening toilette was a far grander and more exciting exercise.

The drawing-room was empty and Tabbie walked over to the big marble fireplace where a blazing fire was burning and held out her hands to it with pleasure. She was joined there a few minutes later by William: he had done his best with his hair, but as usual it was rather like a bottle-brush and his cravat was crooked and his coat crumpled.

"Come here at once," she said smiling. "And let me put you straight."

She had always put William straight ever since he came down from Cambridge. He came over to where she was standing and submitted meekly as her hands patted his cravat into proper folds and smoothed the coat over his shoulders. Without the usual circle of black coats and crinolines to exclude her from the fire-light another man might have thought how lovely she looked in spite of the demure dress, and how pure her features were and how beautiful were her dark eyes. It was not a thought that occurred to William because to him she was just Tabbie, the cousin who was always ready to run about attending to everyone's wants, just as she "put him straight" and with this in his mind he was inspired to ask, "What shall we all do when you get married, Tabbie?"

"It is not an event that seems likely to happen yet," she said crisply. She patted a lock of hair into place and it sprang back again as if on wires, and he went on seriously:

"I shall be leaving for Norfolk early in the morning, long before you are all astir, and I don't suppose I shall be here again before Louisa's wedding in June. I have promised Mamma I shall be here for that."

She was still frowning at his hair. "If you did put any

water on it in an attempt at smoothing it down," she told him, "it was a complete failure. It's as untidy as I've ever seen it."

"Leave my hair alone, Tabbie." There was something on his mind, that had been there since Arnold's cavalier treatment of his cousin had been brought home to him one Wednesday evening by Dr. Ashley's offer of his carriage. "I want to ask you something, and I hope you won't think it impertinent because it is not meant to be."

"Then I am sure I shall not think anything of the sort." She shook her head at his cravat that showed every symptom of twisting itself round again. "What is it, William dear?"

"It's this—do you think you will be happy with Jarrett?"

She forgot his cravat and her eyes met his for a startled second, her hands dropping to her sides. "Why yes, I think so," she said then slowly.

"But—are you fond of the fellow?" he persisted.

"Yes, I am fond of him," she said. "And I think I know him very well—all his little foibles, I mean, as he knows mine. And I think that is as good a basis for a happy marriage as any other—though not perhaps highly romantic." She dismissed the subject with a laugh that sounded a little forced. "And talking of marriage, it is high time *you* were getting married, William. I wish we could find somebody to be your wife now that you have that nice house in Norfolk."

"I am much obliged." He dismissed his misgivings over Arnold and laughed with her. "Is there anybody you have in mind?"

"Well not exactly, but Miss Fulgrove is reputed to be very wealthy."

"That man-eater? No thank you, my dear!"

"Then what about Miss Ashley?"

"I thought we were discussing a wife, Tabbie dear, not a mother. Miss Ashley is at least ten years older than I am."

"That scarcely makes her old enough to be your mother. And my arithmetic is better than yours: she is not much over thirty and you are twenty-eight, so there is not a great deal of difference between you. You must admit that she is a pleasant and a charming woman."

"And dedicated, as her friend Miss Nightingale is. I am sorry, Tabbie, but you will have to direct your match-making elsewhere as far as I am concerned. I would not care to marry a dedicated woman—unless she were to be dedicated to me of course."

And then as Lady Sackroyd came into the room resplendent in velvet and enough jewellery to fill a jeweller's shop window, their conversation was at an end, because almost immediately Tabbie was sent off for a lace handkerchief that she had left on her dressing-table, and William was told to go and put some bear's grease on his hair. By the time they returned to the drawing-room the first guests had arrived.

The Jarretts came with Miss Fulgrove and Mrs. Gaywood in Miss Fulgrove's carriage, which made Mrs. Jarrett very smug all the evening and given to referring to Selina constantly in Lady Sackroyd's hearing as "my kind friend."

Tabbie had hoped to have William beside her at dinner, but he was given over to the "man-eater" and shot her a wry look of dismay as Selina took firm charge of him. She found herself sitting opposite them between Arnold and Dr. Ashley, whose partner was Mrs. Gaywood.

Arnold's attention was entirely given to listening to what William was telling Miss Fulgrove about Jamaica, which he had visited after he left Cambridge, and she could only elicit monosyllables from him. Dr. Ashley, finding his own partner happily engaged with a brother officer of Harry Rawlings' on her left, and annoyed by Arnold's churlishness, asked Tabbie how long William had been in the West Indies.

"Only for a year." Her face lit up and she smiled: she had, he thought, an enchanting smile. "My uncle has an interest in a sugar plantation there." She did not add that poor William had fallen desperately in love with the Rector of Westways' eldest daughter, and it was after she had married Mr. Cray that he had gone off to Jamaica, coming home at the end of a year cured of his love-sickness and as yellow as a guinea. "Poor William. It was his stay in the West Indies that started his interest in drains."

"Were they very bad out there?"

"Neither good nor bad because there were none." Her eyes met his drolly and he laughed and told her that the drains at St. Ursula's were likely now to be put in perfect order, thanks to her cousin's advice.

"How does your sister like working for St. Ursula's?" she asked.

"Very much. She was working for a little while last year with Miss Nightingale in her hospital for sick ladies in Harley Street. There are several such hospitals in and around London and when we came to Kensington Blanche was delighted to find St. Ursula's in Old Brompton, an easy walk from our house. It stands back from the road behind a high garden wall and it used to look out over spacious nursery gardens, but the New Town is spreading so fast that I'm afraid by the end of the year the last of the old gardens will have gone."

"It is a pity that all our green spaces are being gobbled up so fast by the builders. My uncle says it is the result of progress and prosperity, but I regret it all the same. How many ladies are there at St. Ursula's?"

"Eight at the moment, but Blanche is hoping to be able to accommodate more. In the meantime she is endeavouring to collect a band of helpers willing to assist in mending the hospital linen, some of which is in a deplorable state. It was all given to St. Ursula's as I expect you know, but whereas some ladies were generous enough to have new linen supplied a number simply turned out the old worn remnants of their linen rooms. Blanche says though that a great deal could be done with it if she could have the aid of skilled fingers, but the ladies of Kensington have so many bazaars requiring the work of their needles that she has not met with a great deal of response."

"I wonder if my aunt would spare me to help?" Tabbie's brown eyes shone. "I would enjoy it. I heard your sister describing her work in Harley Street the other day to one of my aunt's friends, and I do not wonder that she admires Miss Nightingale. St. Ursula's is for impecunious ladies as well, is it not?"

"Yes. Governesses and poor clergymen's widows and officers' daughter—ladies for whom nursing at home is a financial impossibility."

Here Mrs. Gaywood, aware that she had been neglecting her dinner partner, deserted the handsome young officer on her left in order to engage him in conversation, and having settled that they both considered the air of Kensington to be more salubrious than that of London, she went on to say how much she admired his sister for showing such a practical interest in St. Ursula's.

"I am afraid that an active kind of philanthropy like hers would be beyond me," she went on, with a flash of her eyes at the doctor. "Nothing would induce me to set foot in a hospital, and although I know Miss Ashley is a great admirer of Miss Nightingale I must say that I find it extraordinary, and indeed slightly eccentric, for a lady born to like the rough work of nursing the sick."

"But then Miss Nightingale is a remarkable woman," the doctor said. Mrs. Gaywood glanced at him thoughtfully.

"You have met the lady?" she asked.

"I have had that honour."

"And what was your opinion of her, Dr. Ashley?" Mrs. Gaywood sunk her voice. "Your private opinion I mean?"

"You must not ask me that, my dear lady. I fell under her spell the moment I met her, and so I am hopelessly biased." His eyes went back to Miss Fulgrove: Arnold's attention was still engrossed by her and he wondered if the lady had a living in her gift and that was the reason for his interest. Mrs. Gaywood, having been polite to the doctor and failed to draw his attention to herself, felt that she need do no more. She was free to turn a shoulder on him and ask the soldier beside her if he thought there was real prospect of war with Russia, as the newspapers seemed to predict.

"No prospect at all, ma'am." He was delightfully reassuring. "No need to worry that lovely head of yours over things like that."

It was pleasant to be called lovely, even if one knew it to be totally untrue. Mrs. Gaywood dropped her voice and got on to more personal topics.

Someone else had had his attention drawn to Tabbie that evening and after dinner when William found himself beside his sister Adelaide for a few moments he asked discontentedly if she had no pretty evening dresses that she could give their cousin.

She glanced at him mirthfully. "What makes you think that she needs them, my dear?"

"Oh Addy, where are your eyes? Did you not see her at dinner, sitting there like a little governess among us all? There was Louisa in her new pink dress, and you in this purple velvet—a new one as well, isn't it?"

"It is a new one, William," said Adelaide composedly.

"And very handsome you look in it too. But now turn your head and look at Tabbie standing over there talking to Miss Ashley. She has worn that old grey gown every evening for I don't know how long, and it is so deplorably shabby that I don't know how Mamma can allow her to go on wearing it. Tabbie would be quite a pretty girl, Addy, if only she had a few nice dresses."

"Tabbie will never be *pretty*," Adelaide said with an enigmatic smile. "She is beautiful. That is why Mamma insists on dressing her in dull colours, and that is why she makes her wear her hair braided. 'It is such an unfortunate colour,' she says, as if poor Tabbie can help the colour of her hair. But once Louisa is married she may relent."

"Relent?" He stared. "Addy, you do not mean to tell me that Mamma has deliberately kept Tabbie in the background so that Louisa can shine?"

"Something of the sort." Adelaide touched his arm with her fan. "My dearest William, Louisa is pretty and vivacious and a tremendous flirt. We have all been worried about her, especially when we saw that the men we would have liked to see attracted to her much preferred to talk to Tabbie. Naturally as Tabbie was engaged to Arnold it was perfectly safe that they should do so, but there was no need to emphasise the difference between Louisa and our cousin by dressing Tabitha in dresses that would startle people by emphasising her good looks. I do not know where she gets her manner and those looks from, but they certainly do not come from the Sackroyds. In spite of Mamma's boasting of her children to all her friends, we are a very ordinary set of dumplings. Louisa made a good catch when she became engaged to Harry." She added enviously that she had heard that Harry had bought a house in Belgrave Square.

And then Louisa began to sing and there was no more chance of conversation.

In the few words that Tabbie had exchanged with Blanche Ashley she had been told that if Lady Sackroyd could spare her to help in the linen room at St. Ursula's she would be as welcome as the flowers in May, but when Tabbie raised the matter the next day Lady Sackroyd was more inclined to object than Sir Joseph, who said at once that he thought it would be a very good thing.

"I see no reason why Tabbie should not mend the hospital linen for a few hours, two or three mornings each week," he said. "Will Miss Ashley send her carriage for you, my dear?"

"She will if you cannot spare one, Uncle."

"I do not see why Tabbie should not walk," said Lady Sackroyd. "Jenny can go with her: she is quite a good little maid and Eva's time will be fully taken up with Louisa's wedding clothes."

So it was all settled, and only Arnold chose to be annoyed that he had not been consulted before anyone else.

"You should never have been asked to do such menial work," he said.

"I am only going to mend the linen, Arnold," protested Tabbie.

"So you say." He was still indignant. "You will never set foot in the wards, of course."

"I shall not be required to do so. Miss Ashley says there is an excellent upper nurse there, a Mrs. Morrish by name, who has kindly, clean women for her nurses: she will not have one who drinks in the place. But it is such a small hospital that if my help were needed with one of the patients I could not refuse to give it. It is not like an ordinary hospital, Arnold."

"If it were your uncle would not have allowed you to go there—no doubt Miss Ashley realises that without being told." After a moment he added, "On our way home last night Miss Fulgrove, who had overheard something of what you and Miss Ashley were saying, remarked to my mother that if it was sewing you intended to do for St. Ursula's she thought you might find plenty to occupy your fingers for our future home together."

Miss Fulgrove's impertinence rendered Tabbie speechless for a moment and then she reminded him quietly that they had been engaged for five years. "I have a chest full of linen, all embroidered with my initials, for our future home," she told him. "There is nothing more to be done, and my needle has been at Louisa's service for the past six months."

The following morning after she had called for Blanche and they walked along to St. Ursula's together she asked her new friend why it would have been such a bad thing for her to have nursed patients in the wards of one of the big London hospitals.

Blanche hesitated before replying and then she said gently, "Hospitals, my dear, are for the unfortunates of this world. The patients are usually destitute and sometimes come from a very low section of society. I daresay Mr. Jarrett was thinking of the poor women of the streets who are brought into the hospitals from time to time. One of those that will always receive them is the Royal Free." Tabbie digested this in silence. She knew that the subject of prostitutes was never discussed by her aunt and in fact when Mrs. Gaskell's novel *Ruth* had come out Sir Joseph had refused to have it in the house. He said that if he found a copy he would burn it with his own hands. She was relieved when Blanche changed the subject to Miss Fulgrove, who had refused outright to give any help in the little hospital in Old Brompton. "I think Selina is excellent at organising other people to do charitable work for her," she said, and she laughed. "Mind you, I am not above doing that myself, as no doubt you have noticed! I do spend a great deal of my time with our patients though: the poor old dears are so pathetically grateful for the little things one can do for them—such as writing letters and straightening pillows and feeding them with beef tea and mutton broth. As long as our nurses scrub the floors and keep the rooms clean, and know how to make a poultice and attend to the patients' wants, that is all that can be required of them."

"My aunt told me that Miss Nightingale scrubbed floors when she was at that place in Germany."

"The Kaiserwerth Institution you mean? Yes, Lady Sackroyd was rather horrified I think, and I did not tell her that I thought Miss Nightingale might have emptied bed-pans as well. She is fully capable of it."

"And would you not be capable of it too?" asked Tabbie smiling.

Blanche laughed and admitted that she had indeed done it a few times at St. Ursula's. "When there was an urgent need for it to be done," she added. "But Mr. Jarrett need not fear—such tasks will never be required of you."

Behind the high garden wall of St. Ursula's a gravelled drive led to a long, low building with a lawn in front where an old walnut tree was growing. Blanche led the way to the entrance where the porter touched his hat to her, and they went on into a hall that might have been the entrance hall to a country house. It was square and panelled, with a large fireplace where some apple logs were burning, and a wide carpeted staircase with hand-turned banisters led up to the floors above.

Blanche opened a door marked Private to the left of the stairs, and Tabbie found herself in a large apartment that had been the dining-room in the old days. It was panelled too, and its big bow window looked out on to a walled rose-garden, beyond which the spars and brickwork of the builders on the new houses could be seen.

There was a long mahogany table in the centre of the room piled up with sewing, several large laundry baskets in the window, and shelves of neatly folded sheets and towels and bales of uncut sheeting covered the walls to the ceiling. There was also a basket of clean rags ready for dressing wounds after operations.

That morning was the beginning of many happy hours for Tabbie. It was a relief to get away from the big house in Palace Gardens, with all the busy preparations for the June wedding going ahead, and dressmakers and milliners

for ever wanting to fit dresses and trim bonnets, and
pretty Louisa the centre of it all.

Her neat hems, her almost invisible darns in old pil-
low-cases and sheets made Blanche smile. There was no
need to be quite so particular she told her: hospital sheets
were not the same as those in one's own house, where a
sewing maid was employed to darn and mend household
linen. But as Tabbie could not see any near future in
which she would have a sewing maid to work for her, she
continued to practice her neat darns and hems serenely,
smiling at Miss Ashley's amusement.

Sometimes other of Blanche's friends would join them
in the sewing-room: fashionable young ladies from Bel-
gravia who would come and chatter of the balls they had
been to and the young men they had met, and do a few
stitches of indifferent hemming before their carriages
came to take them on for a drive in the park or an afternoon concert or to listen to the band in Kensington
Gardens on a fine day. Others would come with stately
mammas to visit some old governess who had fallen on
evil times, and Tabbie, sitting in the window by the laundry baskets with her bright head bent over her sewing,
would be acknowledged with a careless nod, and a gay
enquiry, "Are you not Louisa Sackroyd's cousin? When is
William coming back to town?" before they hurried away,
to spend a few minutes with the old friend of their
schooldays, departing with laughing apologies to Blanche
and a gift of money from their mammas for the hospital.

Every day the little maid Jenny called for Tabbie to
walk back with her to Palace Gardens, but on wet days
the doctor's carriage would call and take Tabbie and her
maid home before going back for his sister. Blanche was

amused by his care of her friend and one day as they sat at luncheon together she teased him about it.

"People will begin to talk if your carriage is seen too often taking Tabbie home," she said.

"People will always talk, all the more if there is nothing to talk about." He peeled a hot-house peach for her with care. He was very proud of his hot-house peaches. "Neither Jarrett not Sir Joseph seem to care if your Tabbie gets soaked to the skin." Blanche and Tabbie had been on Christian name terms for some time now but it was rare for him to use anything but the formal Miss Sackroyd when speaking of her and Blanche's amusement increased.

"Nevertheless if you paid so much attention to Selina's health she would think you in love with her," she said.

He halved the peach, removed the stone and handed the fruit to her on a dessert plate. "Now, my dearest Blanche," he said reasonably, "what time have I got for such nonsense as falling in love—either with Selina or—Miss Sackroyd?"

What time indeed? A few minutes on a February evening perhaps, when a hand was put into his and a pair of dark eyes were lifted to his face. A word or two at a dinner-table with all the world listening, a smile across a room at a concert, a softly spoken word of thanks for the use of his carriage on a wet day. No time at all to fall in love. Or maybe all the time that was needed. It was too soon for him to know.

CHAPTER

4

It was about this time that a married niece of Lady Sack-royd's, Sophy Hippenstall by name, moved down to Camberwell from Birmingham. Her husband, Sam, was in the timber trade and having been told in a letter from Sophy's mother of her arrival there, Lady Sackroyd invited her and her five children over one afternoon when she could be sure of not being at home to visitors.

Lady Sackroyd had six sisters, all married, but none so well off as herself, and she liked to keep up a sisterly correspondence with them at a distance, awing them by listing the festivities she attended, the dinner-parties she gave, the grand friends she had made, and what Sir Joseph had recently spent on new carriages and jewels. Her sisters, being good-natured women with husbands whom Lady Sackroyd liked to describe as being in "somewhat humble circumstances," were suitably impressed and kept their distance, all except Sophy's mother, who wrote exuberantly after Christmas that year to say that dearest

Sophy and Sam had been in their house for three months now and she had no doubt that Sophy would like to call upon her aunt. She would bring the children with her—such high-spirited children—and she was sure that Addy's boys and girls would be delighted with them.

Lady Sackroyd did not think Addy would be at all delighted whatever her children might be, and she did not ask her or her family to meet their cousins from Camberwell.

They travelled in an omnibus from Camberwell to Gracechurch Street in the City and there Sam met them and saw them into a cab which eventually stopped in the gravel crescent in front of Sir Joseph's house.

Sophy paid off the cabby and stood for a moment with the children staring up at the Sackroyd "town house." The large square white building, with all its long windows glittering in the afternoon sun, reminded her irresistibly of the glass palace that was rising on the slopes of Sydenham. It had not been built very long and the stucco was not yet coated with London soot, the brass letter-box and knocker in the studded oak door and the heavy brass bell-pull gleamed like silver, and the steps were so white that it seemed a crime to tread on them. And the shrubs in front being but young, and the trees in the small garden only newly planted, the whole house stood up starkly from the park behind it as if someone had thought of starting a country mansion there and forgotten to finish it.

Sophy did not have to ring the bell because her arrival had been noted from glass panels on either side of the door and as she climbed the steps it opened and two powdered flunkeys stood there, dressed most gorgeously in orange plush coats, white breeches and silk stockings. The illusion of entering a glass palace deepened as they followed the flunkeys across the hall, their feet sinking into the Kidderminster carpet, to an enormous drawing-room, where her aunt and Louisa and Tabbie were waiting to receive her. Having negotiated the space between them without tripping over the many footstools and small carved tables loaded with ornaments put there to catch her and her family unawares, Sophy reached Lady Sackroyd at length and was offered her cheek to kiss. The children, having each been greeted by name, were sent off with Tabbie to the school-room on the third floor, where their tea was waiting for them. "A nice school-room tea," Lady Sackroyd told her niece. "With plenty of bread and butter and jam. My housekeeper was sure they would like that." And then while Sophy wondered if her aunt's housekeeper thought that her children did not get such fare at home Lady Sackroyd continued: "We dine at half-past six, and I knew you would want to leave before then, because of getting the children home before it is too late."

"Oh yes," Sophia said happily. "Sam is to wait for us in Gracechurch Street where all the omnibuses collect at that time of night as I expect you know and we shall travel home with him. The coachman let the two elder boys travel outside with him this morning but the three younger children were inside with me. Safer, if rather more smelly." She looked about her admiring the room and Louisa's dress, and her busy tongue was momentarily silenced: Lady Sackroyd told her husband later that she was afraid Sophy was as great a chatterbox as her mother. Presently however she recovered sufficiently to ask if Tabbie was there on a visit.

"Oh no. Sir Joseph—your uncle, my dear—adopted her when she was a baby." Lady Sackroyd touched lightly

on the sad history of Tabbie's birth and the loss of her
parents, and dwelt on her good fortune at having relatives
ready to give her a home, and was surprised when Sophy
said gently that she was very sorry for poor Tabbie. It
must be dreadful, she added, to have no parents, and she
did not know what she would have done if she had none.
Dearest Mamma and Papa were angels: quite the most
wonderful angels in the world. When she learned about
Tabbie's engagement her pity for her increased and she
said she was glad she and Sam had not had to wait five
years before they married.

"Of course Sam would not have done it," she added
laughing. "Dear Sam. We married when he had only two
pounds a week, but it didn't seem to matter. We were very
happy and now that he is making an income of five
hundred pounds a year we feel really rich." She would
have chattered on had not her aunt interposed by telling
her how well Addy had married, and to remind her that
Louisa was shortly marrying Major Rawlings of the Light
Cavalry.

"So Mamma told me," Sophy said, beaming at Louisa.
"I hope you will be as happy as I am, Louisa. I can wish
you no more than that."

It seemed that Sophy was rather stupid and did not understand the position that her Sackroyd cousins held in
the world. Lady Sackroyd said she hoped she liked her
little house in Camberwell.

"Oh yes, we love it there." It had not seemed so little
when they moved there from Birmingham, where they
had lived in a six-roomed villa that had become more
cramped with the arrival of each child. The house in
Camberwell was old-fashioned and roomy and stood in its
own grounds, with a large front garden separated from

the road by a brick wall, in which was a wooden gate bearing the name Laburnham Lodge. There was a still larger back garden, bounded by a wall on either side and a thick, tall hedge at the bottom. On one side a private lane divided the next-door house from theirs, while on the other side the wall was the boundary between them and their neighbours. The children had already found a favourite walk—to Dog Kennel Hill from which they could see the distant outline of what was to be the glass palace at Sydenham taking shape.

When it was time to go and Sophy was taken up to the school-room to collect her family, she found the elder ones in the middle of a paper game, while Tabbie had the youngest, a baby of two, on her lap. They all seemed to be so happy with their cousin that Sophy asked her aunt to bring her with her when she came to see them in Camberwell.

Lady Sackroyd immediately said that neither she nor Louisa would have time to do any visiting before the wedding in June, but Tabbie could go and spend a day with her if she wished, and a visit was fixed for the following week.

A carriage was spared to take her there and to bring her home in the evening, and she was charmed with Sophy's home and touched by the pride with which she showed her over her small domain. The house was old and rambling, the tall chimneys placed at odd angles, the windows latticed, some of those looking on to the back garden being glazed with old green bottle-glass.

The drawing-room and dining-room were separated by folding doors, which as Sophy said happily meant that a number of children could be easily accommodated for a birthday party. The rooms had deep cupboards in them, and though the stairs were steep and narrow the hand-rail was wide enough for sliding down. The kitchen was large and square and stone-flagged, the pantry deep and cool, the scullery owned a pump at the shallow stone sink, and in one corner there was a large copper for the week's wash.

"And wasn't it useful at Christmas time, mum," Sophy's good-tempered cook said, "when we had just moved in and there was all them Christmas puddings to boil?"

At the back of the house fruit trees of all kinds were showing signs of bursting into bud: cherry trees, apple, plum and pear, and the trees were old enough for the older boys to climb. Everything was there to delight the hearts of the children and their parents, and the air of happiness and contentment that radiated through the house charmed and captivated Tabbie, just as she lost her heart to the gay, chattering Sophy and her more silent but placidly smiling husband.

From that day she felt she had a friend with whom she could be as much at home as she was with William or with Blanche Ashley. It was a friendship that was to ripen and endure, and in the meantime with her work at St. Ursula's and the house at Camberwell to escape to, the grandeur of what Sophy called the glass palace in Kensington, and the neglect of Arnold, were easier to bear.

Everything for Louisa's wedding had been prepared with the summer in view, even to the wedding trip to Italy, which was to last three months and on which, to Tabbie's surprise, she wanted her cousin to accompany her.

Here, equally surprisingly, Arnold fancied it was time he put his foot down. "Tabitha," he said wrathfully, "I absolutely forbid you to go to Italy with Louisa and Harry, and I expect you to obey me."

Apart from a gentle carping at nearly everything she did these days he seldom took a firm line about anything, and when she had recovered from her astonishment she said gently, "When we are married, Arnold, you may forbid me to do things and I trust that I shall remember my promise to honour and obey you, but at the moment I am free to please myself and Louisa. She looks on me as a sister, and it is as that sister that I shall go with her on her honeymoon. Harry wishes it too. He is a great deal older than she is, and for all her high spirits she is highly strung and it is only natural that she should want some female of her own family with her in a foreign land."

"And supposing anything should happen while you are away? Supposing I should be offered a living, for example? What shall I do?"

"There is the post," Tabbie pointed out. "And I cannot imagine anything very urgent coming along in that direction that will need my instant opinion, before you accept or refuse it. I know you will do your best just as you know I shall agree to whatever you wish to do. I do not think we can let that stand in the way of Louisa's wishes."

Arnold went off in a huff, and Tabbie let him go, finding excuses for him in her heart. It was natural that poor Arnold should feel as he did, with their own wedding as far away as ever.

Blanche, in whom she confided as they worked together over the hospital linen, smiled and said that she thought Tabbie would make an excellent little gooseberry.

"I went with a cousin on her wedding-trip to Germany," she observed, folding a completed pillow-case and putting it away with others on a shelf. "I found my services were most appreciated during the mornings and afternoons. The evenings were given to opera and the play and concerts, and then I had letters to write, and the bride and bridegroom went to them on their own. I do not think I have ever written so many letters before or since." As she left the linen room for the small office where the month's stores were waiting to be entered in a large ledger, she added, "And you have been so diligent that I am sure we can spare you for as long as Louisa wants you, my dear."

In March, however, everything was suddenly changed by the announcement that France and Britain had declared war on Russia. Harry was told to hold himself ready for orders to embark at short notice, and a June wedding was as much out of the question as a trip to Italy. The wedding was hastily rearranged for early April, immediately after Easter, and a friend lent them a house in Hertfordshire for a week's honeymoon before they returned to the house in Belgrave Square.

Tabbie found herself no longer needed to read aloud to her aunt in the evenings. They had recently been enjoying *The Heir of Redcliffe* and Lady Sackroyd had shed many tears at the more affecting parts. Now, however, her niece's time was fully occupied in writing invitations to the wedding and in acknowledging wedding gifts, and nothing more was said about her accompanying the bridal couple anywhere. Louisa would go with Harry to Hertfordshire alone and snatch what happiness she could from the days that remained before he sailed.

The war was not permitted to cast a shadow over the wedding-day however. The ceremony was held in the parish church and conducted by the Vicar, Arnold being allowed to assist in a minor degree. The bride looked lovely

in white worked silk and Brussels lace, the bridegroom
gallant and handsome though Louisa regretted that he did
not wear his uniform. They were both radiant with happiness and everyone said that the bridesmaids, of which
Tabbie was one, were charming in their white tarlatan
dresses looped up with rosebuds, and wreaths of roses in
their hair.

The wedding breakfast was large, wine flowed, and the
war was not mentioned by anybody. Did the bridegroom
not belong to that most exclusive of brigades, the Light
Cavalry, whose duties consisted almost entirely in attending Royalty when it drove out on its State occasions? It
was not likely that the officers of such regiments, the pre-
cious darlings and sons of so many aristocrats, would be
used in anything but the lightest of actions in time of war.
Even their horses were thoroughbreds and the problem of
shipping them abroad had already necessitated the refur-
bishing of many old sailing-ships, the steam-ships not
being commodious enough to accommodate them. Usually
in such campaigns horses were left behind and fresh ones
obtained on the other side of the water but no horses
could be bought in Constantinople, and so the cavalry
regiments were forced to take their own.

The day itself was lovely enough to quieten any anxiety
that might dwell under the well-bred calm of the bridegroom's parents, and the bride's happiness was not
dimmed by a single shadow. It was a beautiful April day,
sunny and warm as early summer, with the birds singing
in Kensington Gardens and the daffodils bending golden
heads in the park.

After the couple had left for Hertfordshire there was a
ball at the Sackroyd mansion for the young relatives who
had come up from the country for the wedding, and Tab-

bie found herself treated by them as the daughter of the house.

She was still in her white tarlatan dress, the sober grey silk left in the wardrobe upstairs. She looked happy because she was happy, having enjoyed the day that had been such a lovely one for Louisa.

Arnold regarded the tarlatan with disapproval, and when Sophy asked him if he did not think his betrothed looked charming, he replied with a grunt that the dress was too young for her.

"Too young?" Sophy stared. "What can you mean?"

"Well, white you know, with all those flounces and the rosebuds. Quite unsuitable for her age."

"And what about Miss Fulgrove then?" asked Sophy energetically. She had crossed swords with Selina once that day over the exuberant behaviour of her children. "If we are to criticise the ladies' dresses, let us start on hers—an absurdly girlish shade of pink, while the number of flounces on her skirts would put Tabbie's to shame."

"My dear Sophy, Miss Fulgrove has an air that makes every thing she wears look exactly right."

"Indeed? I hope all the same you intend to ask Tabbie for the first dance even if you do not approve of her dress," Sophy said warmly. "Because if you do not somebody else soon will. There is not a man in the room who can take his eyes off her."

"I shall ask Miss Fulgrove first," Arnold said stiffly. "She is a very important parishioner. Tabbie will understand."

"I hope she will," Sophy said to his departing back, "because I confess that I do not."

Hubert Ashley, who had been listening to this altercation with some amusement, watched rather grimly while

Arnold approached Miss Fulgrove, and then he crossed the room to where Tabbie was sitting with Mrs. Gaywood. "May I have the honour of this dance, Miss Sackroyd?" he asked.

"Dr. Ashley!" Tabbie laughed up at him, surprised, and then her eyes went to Arnold. "But I think . . ."

"There is no need to ask Mr. Jarrett's permission," he assured her. "He told Mrs. Hippenstall just this moment in my hearing that his first duty lay with Miss Fulgrove." He saw Mrs. Gaywood's eyes go to Mr. Jarrett and her friend with a slightly startled air and continued blandly, "Come along, Miss Tabbie. The floor is ours!"

She got up and he slipped his arm around her waist and waltzed off with her at a speed that left her breathless.

"You are an extremely good dancer, Dr. Ashley," she said demurely. "Who taught you to waltz?"

"A lady patient of mine a long time ago. But she was not as light as you."

Tabbie was like a feather, and as his eyes lingered on her glowing face he thought Blanche was right and that he might be losing his head a little. To counter such thoughts he said more soberly, "The next time I dance at a wedding, I suppose it will be yours."

She shook her head. "That is as far away as ever I'm afraid."

"It may be nearer than you think." An old gentleman by the name of Sir John Barrington was standing talking to her uncle, and William had told the doctor, swearing him to secrecy, that a living near West Bassett had recently become vacant and that he had only learned that day that it was in the old man's gift. "When he is mellowed with the Guv'nor's port and Napoleon brandy,"

William said, "I mean to bring Arnold to him, hoping that he will be so—so . . ."

"Mellowed?" suggested the doctor.

"Exactly so. Hoping that he will be so mellowed that he will offer him the living then and there. I do not suppose he will make many bones about it. After all one parson will be very like another to an old gentleman like that."

"We will hope so at all events," Hubert said and wondered if his voice had sounded as unconvincing to William as it had to himself.

"If you tell your sister though, warn her to say nothing to Tabbie until everything is settled," William went on. "I would not like the poor girl to be disappointed after all these years. And Sir John may not like Arnold you know, in spite of having been—mellowed—for which I for one could not blame him."

Hubert agreed and tied by his promise now to William merely asked Tabbie if she thought she would like to live in the country.

"If Arnold could obtain a country living, do you mean? Yes, I think I would." She was surprised, but he saw it was because the idea was new to her. "Yes, I think I should like it very much." She waited for him to say more but tantalisingly he changed the subject to her cousin William and how glad he was that he had managed to tear himself away from West Bassett for a few days. "I understand that the dear fellow has been having his house painted, and from what he told me he was rapidly being poisoned by the smell of the paint."

He returned her to her place beside Mrs. Gaywood at the end of the dance and from the tail of his eye saw William making his way towards Sir John, evidently considering that he had been sufficiently mellowed for him to bring Arnold to his notice. But when after having talked to the great man for a little while he looked round for Arnold, he could not be found.

Miss Fulgrove had developed a headache with the heat in the rooms and she had ordered her carriage after the first dance and she and Mrs. Gaywood had gone home. Arnold had offered himself as their escort and the offer had been accepted.

CHAPTER
5

After Arnold Jarrett had left them that night Mrs. Gaywood lingered awhile in the drawing-room, and not being willing to go to bed just then, she started to speak to her friend about something that was on her mind, and had in fact been disagreeably impressed on it during his company in the carriage coming home. There was an ease about the young man when he talked to Selina that had almost bordered on the impertinent.

"Selina," she said. "I feel I must utter a friendly warning and I hope you will not take it amiss."

"A warning?" Miss Fulgrove lifted an eyebrow. "Why, what have I been doing, Julia?"

"It is what Mr. Jarrett has been doing."

"Mr. Jarrett?" Miss Fulgrove's voice was deliberately light. "What can you mean?"

"I think he has fallen in love with you," said Mrs. Gaywood bluntly.

"Oh nonsense!" Selina laughed. "He is engaged to marry Tabitha Sackroyd."

"He may be engaged to her, but he is not in love with her. Every look he gives you, every word he speaks gives him away. I blame him for his presumption while I cannot help pitying him for it, and I think you should be more careful not to encourage him."

"My dear Julia, you are imagining situations that do not exist. You know you have always been a romantic, whereas I am all matter-of-fact common sense. Mr. Jarrett is glad of my advice in parish matters and that is all. If Tabitha Sackroyd were of more use to him in that direction instead of employing her time mending ragged sheets at St. Ursula's, he would not dream of enlisting my help."

Mrs. Gaywood tried to remember any pieces of advice to do with the parish that had been asked or given by the two people concerned that evening and could not remember one. "I hope you are right," she said doubtfully. "But I wish you had not persuaded him to refuse that living in Kent last week. I wonder if he told Sir Joseph that it had been offered to him?"

"I can tell you then that he did not, for he told me so, and I did not blame him for it. A wretched living in a small Kentish hamlet, a damp vicarage and a tiny church and only two hundred souls to look after. It is not the sort of place for Mr. Jarrett's energy and talents, Julia. He would have been lost there."

"All the same, would it not have been wise to let him discuss it with Sir Joseph? He might have had suggestions that would have improved the vicarage if not the living. He has some quite influential friends."

"I have told you, Julia, old Mr. Prince cannot possibly

last much longer: he is over ninety and when he goes I have only to say the word to my brother Walter and the living will be Mr. Jarrett's. It is a large living, as you know, in a thriving suburb, with an excellent modern vicarage and a new red-brick church of the latest Gothic design. The stipend is excellent, and Walter only put the old gentleman into it because he thought a nephew of ours would take it when he left Cambridge. But you know how young men are: he must go and fancy himself not cut out for the Church, and so the old man is still there. Walter will be very glad to have it taken off his hands by Mr. Jarrett when the time comes and it is just the sort of living that he deserves. I had no hesitation in telling him so when we were discussing it the other day."

"It is a pity that you did then, my dear. He needs no encouragement to think well of himself: he has a very good opinion in that direction already."

"I think you are being very unkind to Mr. Jarrett."

"And you are being far too kind to him, my dear. If you will not listen then I will save my breath, but for little Miss Sackroyd's sake as well as for his own I think you should practise more reserve in your manner towards him."

"Tabbie Sackroyd is a milk-and-water little miss, not nearly good enough for him. It was too bad of her relations to throw her at his head as they did."

"From what I hear he was as anxious to become engaged to her at the time, and five years is a long time to wait. Miss Sackroyd might have been quite happy to start her married life in a Kentish village." And then as Miss Fulgrove did not reply she continued curiously, "You are not surely considering whether Mr. Jarrett's affections could be transferred from Miss Sackroyd to yourself?

Even with Walter's living in prospect I cannot see you as a clergyman's wife."

"And it is very wrong of you to make such a suggestion." Miss Fulgrove looked seriously annoyed. "I have no designs on Mr. Jarrett and you are as aware of it as I am. He is free to marry whom he pleases and when he pleases: my only wish is to further his best interests."

Mrs. Gaywood remembered Selina's brother having once said that his sister always liked to have a number of young parsons round her skirts. "Selina's tame cats" he called them. She had been angry with him at the time, but there may have been a grain of truth in what he said after all.

"What would you do all the same if Mr. Jarrett were to break his engagement to Tabitha Sackroyd and propose to you?" she asked.

"Such an occasion would never arise." Selina tossed her head contemptuously. "Mr. Jarrett knows his place."

"I wonder if he does? He might imagine, poor man, that his place is by your side. And after your easy manner with him tonight and in the carriage coming home it would scarcely be his fault if he did."

"Oh this is too much. I shall not listen to you in this mood. You are quite insufferable. Good night, Julia!" And Miss Fulgrove lighted her bedroom candle and went upstairs.

Mrs. Gaywood remained where she was for a little while before she followed her: as she reached Selina's door she hesitated a moment, wondering if she would go in and talk over the day's events as they usually did while Selina's maid was getting her ready for bed, and then she decided against it. Selina was spoiled, with more money than was good for her. It did her no harm to have an occasional scolding, and at heart she respected her friend's judgements even if she did not always follow her advice. Mrs. Gaywood could only hope that some of her comments that night had found a mark,

Certainly for the next week or two Selina did not go out of her way to summon Mr. Jarrett to her house, and when Arnold called on his own account she was careful to include Julia in their discussions, keeping rigidly to parish matters. And once she had even said that she was out.

The shadow of her bounty still hung over the parish however, and one day when he happened to meet her walking with Mrs. Gaywood in the park, nothing could be more enthusiastic than her enquiries as to how the penny readings were progressing, and her wish that she had been able to continue the good work herself if there had not been so many calls upon her time. But she was sure that Miss Capp and Miss Knagg were all that could be desired.

Her kindness in fact and the renewed sweetness of her smiles dwelt with Arnold after they had parted, and he found himself storing away in his memory a treasure trove of every word she had spoken and every look she had given him until their next meeting.

Mrs. Gaywood became once more extremely uneasy about the situation, and although she did not discuss the subject the very fact that Selina challenged her to say that she had not behaved well on that occasion made her more uneasy still.

During the week that followed the wedding Tabbie had little time to think of anyone but her aunt, who made almost incessant demands on her. She declared that she felt

Louisa's departure keenly and that she depended on Tabbie to lift her spirits, and to accompany her on her afternoon drives and on her visits to Louisa's new home, where she cross-examined the housekeeper and made sure that everything would be ready for the Major and his bride when they returned. Even Arnold took a back place as Tabbie tried to distract Lady Sackroyd's thoughts and at the same time prevent her from making an enemy for life out of Louisa's housekeeper.

At the end of the week Augustus's wife invited them to dinner in Queen's Square, and knowing that Sir Joseph was always glad to have a talk with his son Lady Sackroyd accepted for him, although she said she must send Tabbie in her place, as Louisa was returning to London on the following day and she wanted an early night.

The evening followed its usual course as far as Tabbie was concerned: her uncle sat long with Augustus over port and brandy in the dining-room, only joining them for tea later on. In the meantime she had to listen to Cecily's complaints about her servants, the neighbourhood, the tradespeople, and her children's health. Augustus, having purchased the house in Queen's Square cheaply and considering that he had good value for his money, saw no advantage to be gained by moving to a more fashionable district just because his younger sister was to live in Belgrave Square. The time dragged on and the evening seemed as if it would never end, especially as over the tea-tray Sir Joseph continued his business discussions with his son. During the drive home to Kensington he was silent and preoccupied, only rousing himself to remark that Augustus was a son to be proud of and he had heard that he was thought highly of in the City.

They arrived at Palace Gardens soon after midnight,

and as the carriage drove on to the stables, a man stepped out of the shadows by the porch and spoke.

"Good evening, Sir Joseph," he said.

"You!" Sir Joseph stopped dead and his niece was alarmed to see the look of horror that crossed his face.

"Yes, me," said the man mockingly. "It is clever of you to know my voice after all these years, but perhaps it has never been very far from your thoughts?"

"I don't know what you mean." Sir Joseph gripped Tabbie's arm with a shaking hand. "Go indoors, my dear, and leave me alone with this fellow."

"But shall I not send the servants?" She glanced at the tall impacable figure uncertainly.

"No. Send nobody. Only do as I say." And then as she still hesitated, "Damn you, girl, go!"

She ran up the steps and the oak studded door closed behind her.

"I saw in *The Times* newspaper that you had married off one of your daughters," said the stranger. "Did you train her by swearing at her?"

"What do you want?" Sir Joseph glared at his enemy, furious and afraid as well, and a passing constable, hearing his raised voice and thinking he might be in trouble with a night prowler, pushed open the gate and made a leisurely way towards them, his boots crunching on the gravel.

"I want nothing from you," said the visitor contemptuously. "You took everything I had years ago when your arrogant cruelty killed the woman I loved. I came out to Kensington tonight to see for myself the style in which you live—which would be very different if the world knew you for the rascal you are. You were too strong for me years ago, but you are not too strong for me now, and the day will come when I shall be able to even the score between us. I only hope it will come quickly."

"You—you . . ." Sir Joseph spluttered and fell silent as the constable arrived.

"Evening, Sir Joseph," he said, and his eyes as they probed the stranger were sharp and keen. "I hope this man is not—threatening you in any way?"

"No. It is quite all right thank you, constable. Good night." And Sir Joseph hurried away up the steps after his niece.

The stranger stood looking after him with a smile and the constable said reprovingly, "I 'ope sir, you've not been molesting Sir Joseph in any way? He is a very 'ighly respected gentleman, round these parts, is Sir Joseph Sackroyd."

"I am sure he is." The stranger's smile deepened. "I would have liked to knock him down, mind you, but that is neither here nor there." His voice was quietly mocking but it was the voice of a gentleman and the constable was puzzled.

"I wouldn't go about saying things like that if I was you, sir," he protested. "It would go agin the grain to 'ave to run you in or otherwise take you up for threatening be'aviour."

"It would go equally against the grain for me to be run in or otherwise taken up," said the other pleasantly. He eyed the burly form of the constable with his leather hat and the truncheon at the belt under his coat with amusement. "Do not look so worried. I shall do nothing to disturb the peace, and it is not I but his conscience that has threatened Sir Joseph over the years since we last met. I did not mean to say as much as I did, but fortunately we are a free nation and can say what we like. Subjects can insult their sovereign and the poor can insult the rich and so on. That is why we have not had a revolution here in England. You look puzzled. I beg your pardon. I talk too much. Is there a cab rank in the High Street?"

"Why yes, sir, opposite the new Vestry." Something in the gentleman's bearing made the constable offer to walk with him down Palace Green and summon a cab for him. "Are you going far, sir?"

"Cavendish Square."

"Oh then you'll 'ave no difficulty there." They reached the High Street and turned right past the church and a cab soon separated itself from the rank. The constable found himself thanked and a sovereign was slipped into his hand, a thing that Sir Joseph had never done in his life, not even at Christmas when he was off duty. He wondered as he returned to his beat what it was that had made Sir Joseph look so frightened when the gentleman spoke to him. He hadn't half got up them steps quickly and the doors shut between them, but the gentleman had made no attempt to follow him. He just stood there smiling in a queer, bitter sort of way, as if for all his talk of getting even with him he knew that whatever had been done in the past could never be undone.

Very grand was Sir Joseph Sackroyd with his horses and his carriages and his lady driving about in her jewels and furs and bending her head in acknowledgement of a touched cap with never a smile on her face.

Not real gentry, Sir Joseph and his lady, although there had been some real gentry at that grand wedding of theirs a week ago. You knew them at once, though the paint was peeling off their carriages. The coats of arms were there under the peeling paint, and the jewels on the ladies' shabby dresses were finer than my lady's, just as their gentle manners and their charming smiles made you feel you was an equal, as that gentleman did tonight.

CHAPTER
6

Louisa was back and her delight in her house and her husband made Tabbie a little wistful and Lady Sackroyd almost as pleased as her daughter. Tabbie now found time again for St. Ursula's, though visits to Camberwell were still out of the question, the carriage always being required elsewhere.

After Louisa had been back a week however Sir Joseph told Tabbie that he would like to speak to her in the library as soon as she had finished her breakfast, and she obeyed the summons in some surprise, wondering what had happened to make him so unsmiling and stern.

The thought came into her mind that it might have something to do with the man who had accosted him on the night they had been to dinner with Augustus, but as he had not mentioned the episode since and she had not dared to say anything about it she did not think it could be that.

He received her with his usual kindliness and told her

to sit down. She anticipated bad news and wondered if Harry had had his marching orders and that her aunt did not know of it yet, but what he had to say was something quite different and totally unexpected.

"I conclude that Arnold has not spoken to you, Tabbie, about a Norfolk living that was offered to him?" he said.

"A Norfolk living?" She flushed and her eyes shone. "Oh no. But how delightful. I have heard nothing of it."

"I thought as much." His frown deepened and he went on, "You remember no doubt Sir John Barrington, who was one of our guests at Louisa's wedding?"

Even if he had not been staying in the house it would have been odd if she had not remembered him, because his name had been mentioned in every speech to the bride, to the bridegroom, to their parents, from the bride's father, and from the bridegroom's father, and in fact from everybody else who had felt called upon to propose a toast or make a speech on that occasion. Sir John was a very important man.

"I remember him very well, Uncle," she said, wondering what he had to do with the Norfolk living.

"It seems that during the day William remembered that an excellent living had lately fallen vacant not far from West Bassett and he discovered from a friend that it was in Sir John's gift. The stipend is four hundred pounds a year, there is a large vicarage, and some glebe land let most profitably to a local farmer, while the parishioners include not only Sir John himself, but a number of landed gentry. The village does not necessitate a great deal of parish work and in short it would be an easy life for Arnold and a charming one for you and one that promised betterment on a much larger scale later on. William mentioned all this to me, and I immediately took it up with

Sir John, who admitted that he was looking for a suitable
man to fill the living, as the last incumbent had left to become Dean of one of our big cathedrals. Was it Norwich?
No, I don't think so. Perhaps it was Winchester—or Salis-
bury. At all events I sent William to look for Arnold, but
had had already left, and I suggested that Sir John might
like to accompany me to Mrs. Jarrett's house the following morning and meet her son there. He was pleased to
agree and we walked there directly after breakfast and
found Arnold just going out. He took us into the little
room he calls his study—it is more like a cupboard in my
opinion—and Sir John put the matter to him with the
greatest kindness, being good enough to say how delightful it would be to have a vicar there who would be
closely related to myself."

"But why didn't he tell me?" Tabbie was puzzled.
"Was it because he was afraid to raise my hopes in case
nothing came of it?"

"Wait, my dear, there is more to come." Her uncle's
tone was so ominous that she waited apprehensively for
what was to come next. "Somewhat to Sir John's surprise
and my own astonishment—knowing how long he had
been waiting for a living—Arnold asked if he might have
a week in which to consider it, a request to which Sir
John at once consented, thinking as I did that perhaps another living was in the wind. Arnold never consults me
about such things. Yesterday, however, I had a letter
from Sir John asking if Mr. Jarrett had decided to take
the living, as he had another applicant in view. I could see
that he was seriously annoyed and so was I. Arnold had
asked for a week in which to consider it, but he had
not—as far as I knew—mentioned it to you, and it
seemed he had not troubled himself to write to his pro-

spective patron though the week was long past. I summoned him to come and see me and he came yesterday
afternoon while you were out driving with your aunt, and
when I questioned him he had the impertinence to say
that he did not care for Norfolk, he had no idea of bury-
ing himself in a country living, and that he intended to refuse Sir John's offer."

"Oh no!" Tabbie's dismay and disappointment were so
great that she could have cried.

"I can appreciate your feelings, my dear. I was to say
the least of it utterly dumb-founded. I could only presume
that he had the offer of another living, and I asked him if
he could tell me where it was situated. He hummed and
ha-ed a good bit and then said he was not at liberty to
say, but that certain influential friends had lately promised
him an excellent living near London directly it should fall
vacant. Do you know who such friends may be, Tabbie,
and do you know where the living is? Because I'm hanged
if I do."

Tabbie shook her head. Her thoughts went to Miss
Fulgrove but she was too disappointed and hurt to say
anything.

"I asked him if he did not think the certainty of a good
living today was better than one that might become vacant—and might not—in the future, and he only smiled
and did not reply. I then asked if he did not think he
should at least talk it over with you before he made up
his mind. I reminded him that you had been engaged to
him for five years already, to which he replied with the
greatest assurance in the world that nothing would be
gained by talking about it as he was determined to refuse
the living, and that all decisions as to his future must in

his opinion be made by himself alone." He paused and took a quick turn about the room, going on:

"I am most gravely displeased with Arnold and I told him so. He will no doubt call upon you in the course of the day to explain his actions—indeed, I told him that I should expect him to do so. Not that I wish to hurry your wedding, my dear. Your aunt and I are glad to have you with us, and now that Louisa has her own home I know your aunt will depend on you more than ever for companionship."

"Thank you, Uncle. You are very kind. I need not tell you how much I appreciate your kindness and affection." She got up and kissed him with tears in her eyes. He returned the kiss restrainedly, looking a little uncomfortable, as he always did under any demonstration of affection, particularly from Tabbie. "Bless my soul," he said, patting her shoulder, "you are a good girl. When Arnold comes mind you give him a good drubbing. You are too gentle with the fellow, Tabbie."

After she had left him he sat for some time frowning into the fire. It was maddening that Jarrett had frustrated a prospect that had been to everybody's good. Once married and settled in Norfolk Tabbie would have been off their hands: she would no longer be in his house reminding him of what he wanted to forget.

As Arnold had not put in an appearance by four o'clock Tabbie swallowed her pride and set off with Jenny for Edwardes Square, where she found Mrs. Jarrett alone in her dining-parlour busy cutting out flannel petticoats for the poor people of the parish.

Off the High Street that resembled the pleasant main street of any country town, there was a district known to the residents as the Rookery. There were about a hundred

houses there into which were crammed a thousand
people, mostly Irish bricklayers and women who worked
in the market gardens. The district had long been a
nuisance to the residents of Kensington: in the mornings
it was not so noticeable, but in the evenings its inhabitants
would pour out to mingle with the other more respectable
people, the ragged and dissolute looks of the men and
women and the bare feet of the children presenting a
sharp contrast to the well-dressed, well-fed families that
resided in the picturesque old houses in the High Street. It
was from this district that the children came to the penny
readings, understanding nothing except that their small
starved bodies would eventually be refreshed with the
buns and cocoa supplied by Miss Fulgrove's benevolence.

Mrs. Jarrett greeted Tabbie with the off-handedness of
one who is always busy and said that she did not know
when Arnold would be in.

"The poor fellow works so hard," she complained,
"that he never has a moment to himself. I know this must
be difficult for you to understand, dear. People who live
in large houses with plenty of servants to wait on them
have to search for objects to keep themselves occupied."

Tabbie guessed this to be a hint at her work at St. Ursula's and let it pass. "I was hoping he might find the time
to come and see me all the same," she said quietly, "if only
to tell me about the Norfolk living that was offered to
him a fortnight ago. But it appears that he refused it
without question and without consulting me at all. It did
not seem to occur to him that I might like to live in the
country."

"Arnold is not one to put material gains before spirit-
ual ones," said Mrs. Jarrett piously. "He feels that his

place is among the poor—not among the wealthy squires of Norfolk."

"He told my uncle that certain influential friends had promised him an excellent living near London directly it should fall vacant," Tabbie said with a directness that made her future mother-in-law look at her with a hint of anxiety in her small eyes. "If it is true, it is the first I have heard about it."

"Well of course it is true—I mean, it is not for us to question the truth of anything that Arnold says." Mrs. Jarrett was suddenly flustered. "And if you intend to wait for him you may help me cut out these petticoats. Miss Fulgrove provided the flannel—the very best quality though I told her it was not necessary and that an inferior quality would have done as well for the Rookery. But she is so good-hearted: she grudges nothing."

Tabbie thought that if Miss Fulgrove grudged nothing she might have spared a little of her time to cut out and sew the flannel herself rather than leave it to other people. But she could not criticise Selina: it was the one road that led to acrimonious quarrels with Mrs. Jarrett, if not with Arnold, and it was a subject she did not wish to pursue. Fortunately Mrs. Jarrett did not seem inclined to pursue it either.

"I am sorry you have to bring Jenny with you when you come," she said, the note of complaint back in her voice. "She is not nearly such a nice girl as Eva, and she is not good for my Polly. She gossips and puts ideas into her head. Eva always knew her place and never encouraged Polly to look above her station."

And then fortunately Arnold came in to deliver her from his mother, and he was so pleased to find her busy with Selina's excellent flannel that he kissed her quite warmly. His mother had the tact to leave them alone and when the door closed behind her he said that now Louisa was gone he did not suppose she would have time to continue mending the hospital linen.

"My uncle has told me about the Norfolk living, Arnold," Tabbie said, ignoring the hospital linen. "It is that that has brought me here."

"Oh," he said carelessly. "Yes, I suppose he would tell you about it, though it is no business of his."

"No business of his?" She tried to control her indignation. "Is it not my business either?"

"I do not see that it is anybody's business but mine," he replied calmly. "The living was offered to me and I have refused it and there is the end of the matter."

She could scarcely hide her anger. "I would remind you that when there was the question of my accompanying Louisa to Italy you expressly forbade it 'in case you should be offered a living and wished to consult me about it'. And yet here is an excellent living offered you while I am here, only the length of the High Street away from this house, and you did not think it necessary that I should know. I am twenty-three now, Arnold, not the silly girl of eighteen who first got engaged to you. Then you might not have felt called upon to consult me on matters of importance—although I seem to remember that in those days you liked to tell me your thoughts and dreams of the future that we were to share." She broke off, trying to steady her voice. "It seems there is someone else now more worthy of your confidence."

"I don't know what you mean." He tried to laugh it off but his eyes were uneasy and did not meet hers, and she said steadily:

"Arnold, tell me that Miss Fulgrove had nothing to do with your decision against taking that living?"

"Of course she had nothing to do with it. As if I would go to a woman for advice on matters of that sort." She did not believe him but there was nothing for it but to leave the unhappy business where it stood and go home. There were tears in her eyes, however, and for a moment he was touched and tried to make amends.

"I refused that living for your sake as well as for mine, Tabbie," he assured her. "I did not want my wife to be buried in the country where she could be no help to me. There is nothing going on in country districts and I am not sufficiently fond of society to wish to join in endless dinner-parties and breakfasts and things of that sort. I could not afford anything better than a cob to ride, and hunting would be out of the question, and in short I should not enjoy the life at all and neither would you. The country squire, hard-drinking, hard-riding, that your Cousin William seems to have taken to, and the managing squire's lady, are not types that we could admire or wish to make our friends."

"But, Arnold, it would have meant that we could have got married," she said gently.

"If that was all I had wanted I would not have hesitated," he said scornfully. "But I hope my mind is set on higher things—as I am sure yours is, Tabbie. We are both young enough to wait a little longer, and Miss Fulgrove's brother has a good living in his gift. The present incumbent is over ninety and when he dies and the living is free Miss Fulgrove has promised she will tell her brother that he must offer it to me. She says that the old gentleman is three parts senile already and cannot last much longer."

So Selina was the influential friend that he had men-

tioned to her uncle and from whom he was expecting so
much, and while she stood there silent and unhappy he
went on cheerfully, "I am glad you came this afternoon,
Tabbie, my dear, because I wanted to speak to you about
our Wednesday evenings. I think I will have to give them
up until your uncle is in a better frame of mind. He said
some very undeserving things to me yesterday, and if he
did it again I might lose my temper and tell him that he
is not quite the important person he thinks himself to be,
which would not be very becoming to my cloth. I am
sorry to speak thus of your relations, Tabbie, but his
remarks were quite unjustified."

She was too sick at heart to protest any further, or to
defend her uncle in the face of Arnold's complacency,
and she sent for her maid to accompany her home.

She did not offer her cheek to Arnold for a farewell
kiss and neither did she hold out her hand.

CHAPTER
7

At the end of April Louisa gave her first dinner-party and Harry's parents came up to London for the occasion, because news had reached them that their son's regiment was to sail for the east in May. It seemed that the notion that the Light Cavalry would not be required on active service had been a mistaken one.

Louisa, though secretly frightened to death, put on a brave face that surprised and touched Tabbie. It was unlike her frivolous, flirtatious cousin to suppress her feelings, especially when she had been married for so short a time. But she cheerfully directed Harry's servants as to how to get their master's uniforms ready and all the things he would need, such as camp stools and folding tables and a camp bed, and it was only after the Guards regiments had marched away, with bands playing and drummers drumming and the crowds cheering the splendour of the uniforms as they marched through London on their way to embark, that she gave way to tears.

Harry and his servants, his horses, his camp bed and his folding tent had gone, but although Lady Sackroyd implored her daughter to come home she clung to the house in Belgrave Square. The loss of the troopship *Europa* by fire on the last day of May, when it was two hundred miles out from Plymouth, did not lessen her apprehension of the dangers that threatened her beloved Harry, and she was selfishly relieved that it was the 6th Dragoons who had suffered and not the 13th. As Tabbie accompanied her to Kensington Gardens to listen to the band that played there on Sunday afternoons she told her that she could not possibly imagine what she was going through, because nobody who was not married could. "If only Mamma would be like Harry's mamma and keep up her spirits," she added fretfully, "I would find it easier to keep up mine."

Tabbie did her best once more to keep up her aunt's spirits, but it was an uneasy summer in England that year and the gloom cast over the nation in May by the Day of Solemn Fast, Humiliation and Prayer was not relieved until the opening of the Crystal Palace at Sydenham in June.

Sir Joseph had purchased tickets for himself and his wife informing Tabbie graciously that she would be free to accompany her aunt on the days when he did not use his ticket and if Louisa did not wish to avail herself of it. On the day of the opening however he produced day tickets for Tabbie and William, who was in London for the occasion, and for Sophy's mother, who was staying with them for a few nights before going on to Camberwell. The Jarretts had been included in the party, although Tabbie half-wished they had been omitted: her uncle still treated the young man with considerable coldness and it made such a meeting embarrassing. Here, however, William exerted himself to restore harmony, and as they all collected in the hall before starting out he brought Arnold and Sir Joseph into actually exchanging a few words, although it was only to comment on the weather.

The larger of the Sackroyd barouches accommodated Sir Joseph and Lady Sackroyd and her sister and William, while in the smaller one Mrs. Jarrett and Arnold, Louisa and Tabbie, were travelling, much to Mrs. Jarrett's annoyance. She considered she had been slighted by not being included in the first carriage, and found fault continually with the smaller one. Her feet were cold—she thought the carriage doors did not fit well enough and there was a draught at the hinges. She felt every bump in the road: the springs probably required renewing. Could Tabbie look behind them and see if Dr. Ashley's carriage was in sight? She had heard the Ashleys were going and it would be a comfort to know that a doctor was near if he were required. Travelling for long distances in a carriage sometimes brought on palpitations, she found.

The Hippenstalls had not been invited and when Tabbie wrote to Sophy saying that she wished they could be with them and her mother, Sophy replied that they would be far happier going by themselves later on in the summer. *"One day when Sam has a holiday, we shall go to Sydenham by train and we shall mix with the crowds and suck peppermint and enjoy ourselves enormously, much more than we could do under dear Aunt Aggie's eye. But I am glad Mamma is going with you, in case we are not able to fit in our visit to Sydenham while she is in Camberwell."* So wrote Sophy in her careless happy way, her contentment with her lot bubbling over: nothing ruffled her and she envied nobody.

The day was one of bright sunshine with a refreshing breeze and as they had their first view of the new building at Sydenham with the sunlight glittering on the glass, it looked like a palace from a German fairy tale. Indeed, so splendid and beautiful a building had arisen there that it was hard to remember that only a month ago nobody had expected it to be ready in time.

Arnold was sitting beside Tabbie, opposite Mrs. Jarrett and Louisa, and all the way he had steadfastly resisted attempts on Tabbie's part at drawing him into Louisa's light-hearted chatter. At last she gave up trying to coax him out of his sulks and talked to Louisa herself instead.

"I wonder if this glass palace will degenerate as the Great Exhibition did?" she said.

"You mean—all those crowds and omnibuses and cabs?" said Louisa: "Do you remember the day when William took us and we were nearly lost and how frightened I was? We seemed to be surrounded by loud voices and hot red faces and stalls and dogs and penny trumpets and policemen and makeshift public houses. It was quite odious."

"My dear Louisa!" Arnold found his voice for the first time in order to crush Tabbie's cousin. "Those public houses sprang up to cater for the workmen on the Exhibition, as they have sprung up here I notice. Naturally you ladies do not glance at such places, but I assure you there are many more public houses than I remember seeing the last time I came to Sydenham."

Louisa cared nothing for public houses as she looked ahead at the palace, while Tabbie wondered if all such conceptions as full of lofty sentiment and dazzling ideals as Prince Albert's had been, were bound to degenerate when everyday occasions crowded in on them. She remembered how in 1851 every one had said that a new friendliness would exist from that day forward among the nations, that it would in fact put an end to war, all the old enmities and jealousies being stilled for ever, and yet here we were only three years later, at war with Russia.

Arnold was watching the lines of carriages that were following theirs, and she wondered if he remembered the June day five years ago when they had become engaged and she had put her hand in his and raised her face for his kiss. It had seemed to her then that life stretched in front of them sparkling with happiness and sunshine, as this great glass palace was sparkling in front of them now.

In Hyde Park turf and trees had gone back to their old appearance and the Exhibition buildings had gone, much to the relief of the suburban aristocrats who lived about the park, and a memorial was to rise in the proposed new National Gallery and schools of arts and sciences, and rooms for the exhibition of sculptures, planned for the grounds of Gore House and beyond. But what memorial would rise for this new Crystal Palace in years to come? With its walls of glass and the sparkling fountains set in gardens hedged about with flower beds, with its terraces and flights of steps, and man-made lakes with stone effigies of pre-historic beasts.

The opening ceremony was to be performed by the Queen in the presence of at least forty thousand people. Around the dais were to be gathered the magnates of the land, ministers of state, the primates of Canterbury and York and Dublin, and many other important people. The Queen and Prince Albert were to arrive at three o'clock and as they entered they would be preceded by Sir Joseph Paxton and Mr. Laing, and with the Queen were to be the young King of Portugal and his brother the little Duke of Oporto, the Prince of Wales, the Princess Royal, Prince Alfred, Princess Alice, the Duchess of Kent and Princess May of Cambridge. The National Anthem would be sung by massed choirs, and it was all to be very spectacular and splendid. It was said that Clara Novello herself was to be one of the soloists.

As the Sackroyds arrived servants in the Crystal Palace livery hurried forward to help the party to alight and to conduct the carriages to the stables. Other carriages were arriving every minute now, the occupants cheerful and happy and everywhere there was an air of holiday. The men were all in evening dress and the ladies in light dresses, with pretty bonnets covering well-dressed heads.

Tabbie was not surprised that the day was too warm for Mrs. Jarrett, the crowds too dense for her comfort, and that she felt fatigued by the drive. Louisa left them to her grumbles and joined her parents and William and their aunt, and Arnold took no notice of his mother's complaints, his attention still being centred on the carriages that had followed theirs. Mrs. Jarrett was forced to hang on to her future daughter-in-law's arm as she asked plaintively if it was far to go before they reached their seats, and added that she did not fancy sitting for hours in that gigantic greenhouse.

It had been just the same when Lady Sackroyd had procured them tickets for the Corridor, so that they could see the ladies going to one of the Drawing-Rooms at Buckingham Palace. There had been endless draughts that Tabbie was required to combat with shawls, there had been too long a wait which she had found exhausting, and although she admitted that the ladies' dresses and jewels were very fine, she said she had little interest in such things. It was extraordinary how easily Mrs. Jarrett could succeed in spoiling an occasion.

Tabbie let her grumble on while she looked back at the view, which was exceptionally fine.

The great glass palace had been built on the summit of gently rising ground, five miles to the south of London, and instead of being encircled by the trees of Hyde Park it had a magnificent view of London, only partially obscured by the pall of smoke that hung over it from its thousands of chimney pots. Tabbie could see the line of the Thames shining in the summer sun, as far as the White Tower, and beyond it the masts of the shipping stretched like a forest to Greenwich, while beyond Greenwich there was a great expanse of water on which ships were moving to and from the estuary. Then to the south and east of the palace there was a wide prospect over the valleys of Kent and Surrey, rich in orchards and pasture, and Tabbie was turning to Arnold to ask him if he could put a name to some of the hamlets and church spires that rose from the widely scattered clumps of trees when he suddenly thrust his mother's reticule into her hands and hastened away to offer his help to the occupants of a carriage that had just arrived. In it were seated Miss Fulgrove and Mrs. Gaywood and Mr. Walter Fulgrove and his wife.

Having achieved his object in reaching the carriage before the servants could get to it Arnold officiously told them that he would attend to this lady himself, and was only stopped in time by Miss Fulgrove who told him rather sharply to desist.

"Do not send them away, I beg, Mr. Jarrett," she exclaimed. "Unless you are prepared to show my coachman the way to the stables yourself."

Arnold fell back, abashed, and the servants came forward to take his place and assist the lady and her party from the carriage.

"Who is Selina's tame cat?" asked Walter Fulgrove in a low voice as he followed his sister and his wife and the officious Mr. Jarrett to where Sir Joseph was impatiently waiting for the curate to join his party.

"Our curate," Mrs. Gaywood said in the same subdued tone. "And you are not to call him a tame cat. Selina would not like it."

"You are not telling me that she is serious over the man?"

"Good heavens no. He is engaged to be married."

"That is one comfort at all events."

"And what is more," added Mrs. Gaywood with a twinkling eye, "I think Selina has an idea that he might succeed old Mr. Prince when the gentleman finally departs this life."

"You surprise me."

"Has she said nothing to you about it?"

"She has not." Walter Fulgrove's eyes rested rather critically on the back of Mr. Jarrett's shabby black coat. "We shall have to see about it when the time comes, won't we?" he said.

As Sir Joseph approached the Transept he was hailed by Augustus, who was installed there in the Main Avenue with his family.

"What are the colours of your tickets?" he asked. "Not that it matters." He nodded contemptuously towards the many policemen who had been appointed to direct ticket-holders to their seats and were doing their best to discover from tickets that were all colours of the rainbow, where they should put them. "Those fellows have no idea of where they are sending everyone. I have kept four seats for you but I see that four is not enough. You had better come into the row behind us. There are nearly a dozen places vacant there."

Miss Fulgrove and her party were glad to take the four seats in the front row beside Augustus and as his father's party filed into the row behind he turned round to say, "I cannot think why you were not here hours ago. We had to come through the Borough, which is the devil of a place to get through at any time of day, but if your coach-man followed the directions I gave him last week you should have had no difficulty at all. It is the only correct way to come from Kensington."

Sir Joseph assured him that they had come over the Vauxhall Bridge to the Kensington Turnpike and down the Wandsworth Road to Brixton Church, and when they reached the George Canning Tavern they had turned sharp left as he had advised. "But the bridge over that dirty little river Effra is such a narrow one that I was apprehensive for my new paint," he added. "I would not have liked it to be scratched."

"Oh stuff! There's room for two carriages to pass there easily. But I suppose that is why you are late. Your fellow was not to hurry in case he scratched your new paint!" Augustus laughed. "There's excellent galloping ground once you have left the stones though, and you should have made up time there. We came along at a capital pace. If I had not had to wear evening dress I'd have ridden down this morning—just the morning for it and most of it over grass. Clapham Common, Balham Hill, Clapham Park and Tooting Common, and then through the trees to Streatham Common—I would have enjoyed it immensely. But of course dressed up like this we had to use the carriage."

In the meantime the others in Sir Joseph's party had sorted themselves out. Sir Joseph and Lady Sackroyd, her sister, Louisa and William being in the seats immediately behind Augustus and his family, Tabbie and the Jarretts were left to sit where they pleased, which once more gave offence to Mrs. Jarrett. She fidgeted a great deal, saying that she could not see, until the matter was settled by Tabbie giving up her place to her beside Arnold. His only concern was to make sure of a place directly behind Miss Fulgrove, and after Selina had turned to greet Mrs. Jarrett she introduced Tabbie rather pointedly to her brother as the future Mrs. Arnold Jarrett. Walter gave the young man rather more respect: tame cat he might be but he had picked a remarkably beautiful young woman. Tabbie's hair and eyes and features did not escape Mr. Fulgrove and he felt that a further acquaintance with Jarrett and the young lady might be rewarding.

Tabbie in the meantime felt a hand on her shoulder and Blanche's voice said behind her, "I tried to catch your eye when you came in but you would not look at us!"

"I beg your pardon. I was too much occupied to look about me I'm afraid." Tabbie was delighted to have her friend so near and she included her brother in her welcoming smile.

"I saw that you were occupied." Blanche's eyes dwelt for a laughing moment on the back of Mrs. Jarrett's bonnet, a miracle of purple feathers and nodding jet. "Hubert says he is certain we are in the wrong seats. He thinks these are reserved for important people and that we may be turned out."

Dr. Ashley, who had been watching the activities of the bewildered policemen in front of them with amusement mixed with concern, saw the Director hurry into the Nave at this moment and give a horrified glance at the occupied seats before summoning his minions and issuing frenzied instructions. As Hubert had foreseen it was the empty amphitheatre opposite that they should have been occupying, and they were all asked politely but firmly to move across the aisle.

Immediately there ensued an undignified scramble, in which Blanche was almost knocked down as the people behind her tried to push their way out. William, turning his head in time to see what was happening, leapt up to help her, freeing her brother to go to the assistance of Mrs. Jarrett and Tabbie. Arnold's only thought appeared to be to give assistance to the party in front of him, and seeing that Blanche was safe with William Dr. Ashley put one stalwart arm round the tubby little form of Mrs. Jarrett and the other round Tabbie's slender waist, and shepherded them down the gang-way without any hurry.

"We will let the rabble clear first," he told William in a clear voice that had a good carrying propensity. "There are plenty of seats across the way and we shall have as good a view as we have here, and probably a better one if we don't break our arms and legs fighting others for them first."

His words had a calming effect on the people crowding in behind them. Others took them up and repeated them, and the move was made with more dignity and sense.

When they eventually arrived and found seats to their liking in the amphitheatre on the opposite side the ladies' finery had not been ruffled and the gentlemen still re-

tained their hats, although they found themselves far removed from Sir Joseph and his family while Arnold had
vanished.

They discovered him at last on a seat beside Miss Fulgrove in a row some distance below their own.

"That fellow," remarked Dr. Ashley in a low voice as
he waited with William for Mrs. Jarrett to find a place
where she could be sure of an uninterrupted view of the
proceedings, "seems to have eyes and ears only for the
man-eater."

William's eyes followed his to Miss Fulgrove and he
grinned. "I see we think as one," he said, and then, making sure that Tabbie could not hear, he went on, "How
my cousin could ever have engaged herself to marry such
a fellow passes my comprehension. I can only suppose
..." Here he paused and the doctor finished his sentence
for him with some abruptness.

"That love is blind?" he said.

"Exactly so."

Mrs. Jarrett was taking a long time to settle and
Blanche and Tabbie were doing their best to find her a
suitable position and William continued: "Dear little Tabbie. I see she is wearing that dowdy old grey silk dress of
hers again. I do wish Mamma would find her a new gown
or two. But in spite of her old dresses she is so pretty,
isn't she? But of course I suppose you would not notice
things like that."

"Would I not?" said Hubert.

"No, because you only see people when they are ill and
nobody is at their best when they have sore throats and
you take their pulse and tell them to say 'Ah' and that
sort of thing. You could not possibly discover if a person

were amusing to talk to or even beautiful to look at under those conditions."

"No, I suppose not," agreed Hubert. "On the whole I am afraid we doctors are a sadly unobservant lot of fellows."

"You have to be," William told him candidly. "Otherwise you wouldn't be able to cut off people's legs so cheerfully would you?"

"I do not think I have ever cut off anybody's legs," said Hubert. "I am not a surgeon you see. But if I have to do so I hope I may do it cheerfully."

At this point Mrs. Jarrett finally managed to be accommodated in a seat that was not hidden behind too large or too fat or too tall a person, and although she was afraid that the small girl in front of her might fidget she was resigned to the fact that it was the best that could be found. With a sigh of relief Tabbie and Blanche sat down on either side of her while William went to Blanche's right and Dr. Ashley found himself beside Tabbie. She was looking very thoughtful and presently he dived his hand in his pocket and brought out a penny and held it out to her on the palm of his hand.

She laughed. "I am sorry. My thoughts were miles away." She glanced down at the row below them. "Do you know who that gentleman is with Miss Fulgrove?"

"I believe he is her brother."

"I thought he might be." She hesitated. "He is the gentleman who has a living in his gift, and Miss Fulgrove has very kindly promised to keep us in mind when it falls vacant."

"I see." That could be the reason for Mr. Jarrett's interest in the man-eater: Dr. Ashley felt he might have misjudged him. "I presume it is not a London living then?"

"Oh no. I am not sure where it is, but it is not far from London. Miss Fulgrove says it is a well-to-do parish and that there is no quarter there so rough as the Rookery."

"And what do you know about the Rookery?"

Her dark eyes laughed up at him. "Before Addy married, when I was about sixteen, she saw herself as a ministering angel to the Rookery, and my aunt insisted that I should accompany her when she visited that interesting district. I can't say that I enjoyed it very much. Those courtyards!" She wrinkled her nose and he smiled grimly, thinking of the inadequate privies that were never emptied by the landlords until the yards were awash. "The children swarmed round us begging for money."

"They learn the beggar's whine very early in the Rookery."

"Poor little creatures." Her soft voice was compassionate. "And all pouring out the most harrowing stories of mothers dead, or in hospital, and younger brothers and sisters starving."

"Mostly lies, I'm afraid, Miss Tabbie."

"Why yes, because when we had given them all our money they started shouting at us, their favourite question being, 'Yah, does your muvver know yer out?' "

He laughed at her excellent imitation of the small ragamuffins in the Rookery. "And how long did your visits last, may one enquire?"

"Not very long. Our ministering angel caught scarlatina and my uncle forbade us to put our noses inside the district again."

"The question I am most frequently asked by those young ruffians is 'Where did you get that 'at?' followed invariably by the hat in question being knocked into the gutter by a well-aimed potato."

"That is what they do to Arnold. He gets very angry with them."

"He should do as I do and keep his oldest hats—and his oldest clothes—for visiting the Rookery."

"Blanche says you are a great favourite there."

"Blanche is my sister and therefore biased. She is quite mistaken in thinking that I am loved for myself alone. They simply know that they can have my advice and help free whenever they want it, and that is the sole reason for my popularity. They would rather have Dr. Ashley at their bedsides insisting that they should eat good food than be packed off to hospital."

"And am I right in thinking that Dr. Ashley often brings the good food with him?"

"Oh, Mrs. Webb cooks far too much for our household in any case." He dismissed her question in a hurry. "And I cannot bear to see tiny babies starved through carelessness and neglect."

"But if you insisted that they bought the nourishing food for themselves would it not mean less for them to spend in the public houses and the gin-shops?"

"The ethics of such things I must leave to Mr. Jarrett," he said. "And if I'm not mistaken here he is come to see how you are faring."

And there indeed was Arnold, but his face showed no pleasure when he discovered them: he appeared to be extremely annoyed and Tabbie wished ungratefully that he had stayed where he was.

Having settled them all in their new places, Miss Fulgrove was surprised when Arnold sat himself down beside her as if he intended to stay with her party. She had been

grateful for his help but she felt that it was no longer
needed, and that his duty now lay with his own. She
smiled at him brightly and said with some emphasis:

"That was very kind of you, Mr. Jarrett, and we will
not detain you any longer. Your mother and Miss Sackroyd must be wondering where you are."

To her astonishment he did not move or make the
slightest attempt to rise from the seat beside her. "Oh
they will not be troubling about me," he said carelessly.
"William and Dr. Ashley have taken charge of them.
There is no reason why I should move."

"No reason!" Selina gave a little gasp. "I am afraid I
don't understand you, Mr. Jarrett. At least," more coldly,
"I hope I do not."

"Miss Fulgrove, you are angry with me!" He dropped
his voice. "Please do not be angry. I could not resist the
chance of being with you, and I know you will not blame
me in your heart."

This was too much. She glanced at her brother, but
fortunately he had not heard, and she said in tones of ice,
"I would like you to fetch your mother to take this seat
beside me, Mr. Jarrett. It will be better for her than being
so far away up there. Fetch her at once please."

He dare not disobey, and he got up and went to fetch
Mrs. Jarrett, feeling humiliated and frightened and angry.
He knew that he had overstepped the bounds of familiar-
ity that Selina would allow, but he comforted himself with
the thought that it was simply because her brother was
there. When he was alone with her and Mrs. Gaywood
again after he had gone she would be as kind as ever.

Mrs. Jarrett was delighted to join Miss Fulgrove and
although he conducted her there himself he could not win

a glance from Selina, whose attention and concern were centred on his mother.

"Fortunately there was a seat to spare," she told her. "And I was able to keep it for you. Mr. Jarrett has been most helpful and I am sure he will be pleased to rejoin Miss Sackroyd."

Firmly dismissed for the second time and put down in his place Arnold climbed the gangway again and joined the party of four above them. He found they had kept Mrs. Jarrett's place for him behind the fidgety little girl, and between Tabbie and Blanche Ashley, and his sulks were not noticed by anybody.

On one side William was giving Blanche an absorbing account of his house in Norfolk and the prospective draining of his cess-pool, while on the other Dr. Ashley was telling Tabbie the history of St. Bartholomew's Hospital, and as he had started with its foundation by Rahere, minstrel to Henry I, it promised to take a long time. None of them seemed to have time or inclination to include Arnold in their conversation and he felt very ill-used indeed.

He felt more ill-used still when at the end of the day Miss Fulgrove's carriage arrived before Sir Joseph's and she departed with her friends, and did not see or hear him when he said goodbye, so that his hat was lifted to the back of her head.

"It has been a very long day," said Mrs. Jarrett, hanging on to his arm. "Though I must say Mr. Fulgrove was very kind in giving me a little brandy from time to time from his flask. I do not think I could have kept up without it. It was so very warm in there too, was it not, although everyone kept saying that the fountains cooled the air. And the Queen spoke so softly that I could not hear a word she said. But what a very handsome man Prince Albert is. Miss Fulgrove said she could quite understand why the Queen fell in love with him. She made us all laugh very much. And the choirs dressed all in white behind Madame Novello. What a lovely voice she has—like an angel—and in white too. Such a lovely dress. Yes, although it was a long day I must say I enjoyed it."

Her son was sorry that he could not say the same.

CHAPTER
8

In July cholera broke out again in London, striking at the crowded districts of St. Giles's, and in the poorer areas of cities throughout England.

Louisa went off reluctantly to Perle Place, confiding to Tabbie before she left that she was rather frightened of her mother-in-law.

"That gentle little lady?" Tabbie could not believe it. "What is there to frighten you in Mrs. Rawlings?"

Louisa did not answer for a moment and then she said, "Well, you see, she admires you very much, and when I remarked on the 'unfortunate' colour of your hair—you know how we have always laughed about it, Tabbie, meaning no harm—she rounded on me and said it was beautiful hair, that it was auburn, not red, and the colour that Titian loved to paint. And then she said with rather a cool smile, 'If you know who Titian was!' Well, of course I know who Titian was. Not that I like old pictures. They have too many at Perle Place, so dark and gloomy and all portraits of dead and gone Rawlings, looking down their aristocratic noses at poor me."

"I daresay she did not mean to hurt you," said Tabbie soothingly. "And it was kind of her to admire my hair." She laughed. "She is the first person who has had a good word to say for it, isn't she? Was that all she said, Louisa?"

"No. She said you reminded her of somebody she knew years ago and she asked who your father was, and when I said I didn't know . . ."

"You didn't *know*? Louisa!" Tabbie was shocked.

"Oh—well, yes." Louisa was suddenly flustered and went very red. "What I meant to say was that a naval officer called Smith couldn't have been anybody that the Rawlings would be likely to know, would he?"

"No, I suppose not." But Tabbie still looked bewildered and Louisa hurried on:

"And then you see I think he must have been in 'humble circumstances' as Mamma says, because don't you remember when William was staying with a University friend in Cornwall years ago, and you asked him to go and see your mother's grave at—Travennick I think—he couldn't find it, though Papa said it was there. So it proves your father couldn't have been anybody important, Tab, or there would have been an important looking tombstone put up for my aunt, wouldn't there?" And then, as if fearful that Tabbie might dispute this and land her in a further dilemma of explanation she asked when the carriage was coming to take her to Paddington Station and she hoped she would not lose the train, because the Rawlings had arranged for it to stop at Perle Place and they would be vexed if she was not on it.

After Louisa had gone Sir Joseph packed his wife off to

Westways Grange, nervous lest the Rookery might be affected, and Adelaide and her family and Augustus's wife and children went with them. He offered tentatively to include the Hippenstalls but here Lady Sackroyd put her foot down. Camberwell was almost in the country, she told him, she had seen hayfields round about there herself. Nobody could imagine any danger of the fever breaking out in Camberwell, and the Grange was not large enough to accommodate the Hippenstalls as well as all the others. When Tabbie ventured to remark that Kensington was also surrounded by fields, she crushed her by saying that Camberwell had no Rookery to threaten the health of gentlemen's houses. She was quite seriously annoyed when she heard that William had written to Sam offering his family a home at West Bassett for as long as they wished to stay, and she wrote at once to her impulsive younger son to tell him that there was no need for this act of quixotic generosity.

"If you have Sophy and her family at West Bassett," she warned him, *"you will bitterly regret it. I will not have them at the Grange, and if Sam accepts your offer—as undoubtedly he will—I do not think Sophy should come alone with the children. They are very unruly and your house will be Bedlam, as she will only bring a young nursemaid to help her with them. They will upset your housekeeper and all your servants will give notice."*

William countered these threats however by writing to ask if Tabbie could not come with them. She had such a quietening influence on everybody and he knew that she and Sophy were very attached to each other.

Lady Sackroyd read this letter to her husband with fresh dismay. "I am depending on Tabbie to help with all the children at Redhill," she said.

"There is not the slightest need for her to come with us, my dear," Sir Joseph said. "Addy has an excellent nurse and under-nurse, and Cecily has an equally good governess for her children. I see no reason at all why Tabbie should not go to Norfolk."

And so it was arranged, and William was delighted to welcome his cousin with the Hippenstalls when his crowd of young relatives hurled themselves out of the train at the little station at West Bassett and flung themselves upon him, all talking at once and asking a dozen questions without waiting for them to be answered. A train journey was almost the most exciting experience they could have and they went on chattering without ceasing as he packed them into the station wagonette, leaving the luggage to be sent up in the carrier's van later.

"Sam doesn't think the epidemic will last long," Sophy said as they started out through the lanes. "Otherwise I would not have left him. But our doctor thinks it is due to dirt and that it is not a contagious or infectious disease."

"That is what Dr. Ashley says," agreed Tabbie.

Blanche had wanted to leave St. Ursula's in Mrs. Morrish's hands while she went to help Miss Nightingale, who was at the Middlesex Hospital nursing cholera patients. The hospital was crowded out with the poor things, staggering in off the streets. But in the end Blanche had thought her duty to be first of all with her brother. The Rookery had a number of cases already and an epidemic was on the way, while Kensington was emptying fast with people shutting up their houses and making for the country earlier than usual so that Hubert had more time to give to his poorest patients.

"I hope my new bonnet does not smell of straw," chattered on Sophy. "I hung it out of the bedroom window every night for a week before I trimmed it, and when I held it under Sam's nose he said it didn't smell. But then he's so obliging over anything like that."

William assured her that nobody would smell her bonnet and that it could not compete for a moment with all their country smells. "You wait till we reach Farmer Dodd's pig-styes beyond the church," he added, with a grin that made her threaten to take off the offending bonnet and beat him with it.

It was a joy to William to have his cousins there. The weather was fine and warm, and as the house echoed with the children's voices, so did the garden resound to cricket bats and bows and arrows, and kites were flown getting entangled in the trees, while the youngest of Sophy's family was content to sit on the lawn making daisy chains, crooning to himself and being watched over by his nursemaid who, being only fifteen, took her duties very seriously.

There were picnics on the Common up the road, and there were the chickens to feed down in the meadow, and eggs to collect, and the housekeeper's bantams to admire in their separate coops. There were the ducks on the pond, turning turtle with their tails in the air, and there was the old pony to ride on his way back to his stables after pulling the roller or the mower over the lawn, there was a swing, made for them in his carpenter's shop by William who prided himself on his aptitude for turning, and they made him a small white paper cap so that he should look like a real carpenter as he worked. When August came they watched the stooks being pitched like great golden dolls in the harvest fields, and they went blackberrying in the lanes.

On Sundays William took them to church and they behaved so well that he congratulated Sophy on her up-bringing.

"It isn't me or Sam," she explained as they strolled back together across the village green. "We have a beadle at our church in Camberwell. He is a very important gentleman in a blue coat with brass buttons, and a three-cornered hat and a large staff with a silver top to it. The children are terrified of him and sit as still as mice under his stern eye: he has been known to use his staff on boys who misbehave."

One never to be forgotten day they went on an excursion train—ladies taken at half-price to Sophy's delight and Tabbie's indignation—to Yarmouth.

Sophy's children had never seen the sea before and were in ecstasies of wonder and delight. They flung off shoes and stockings and scarcely waited to have their clothes tucked up before racing down to the water's edge and experiencing the novelty of standing there and feeling the warm ripples of the summer waves coming in to cover their bare feet. They collected seashells and seaweed, which they brought back with them to be the despair of William's housemaids, as treasures to be packed with their toys when they went back to Camberwell.

While they were enjoying a picnic luncheon that day a photographer came along and took their photographs, and in a remarkably short space of time had the pictures ready for them to take home, all in neat little ornamental brass frames—one a group of them all, another of the children and Sophy, and a third of Tabbie, sitting on a breakwater with the youngest child on her lap.

Close on the man's heels came a gipsy woman wanting to tell fortunes. William had started a game of cricket with the children on the sands and Sophy and Tabbie were sitting alone when the old woman appeared. She was extremely dirty, her hair in tight, oily plaits, her eyes bead-like in their cunning, whining out that she would tell their fortunes if they would cross her palm with silver.

They tried to send her off without much success, and at last, as Sophy was getting slightly alarmed, Tabbie said that the only piece of silver she had in her purse was a fourpenny bit.

"I'll not refuse a Joey, dearie," said the woman and reluctantly Tabbie held out her hand.

"God bless your pretty face." The old woman made the most of her opportunity. "A lucky face it is too. Here in your hand, my dearie, I see a great fortune, and a great house like a palace and an important gentleman. Very lucky you are going to be, my dearie. You've been poor up till now and living where you should not live by rights, but now your luck is changing and the gentleman who will change it is not very far away. When he finds you he will give you everything your heart can desire."

William, looking up from the game on the sands and seeing what was happening, now came striding up the beach to send her away, and the old woman departed while Sophy laughed about the fortune she had seen in Tabbie's hand.

"Certainly she did not guess it very well," agreed Tabbie, but as she was wearing a plain grey cotton dress and a plain straw bonnet maybe the old woman had taken her for a governess. She wondered if she promised all such young women the same fairy-tale fortune—an important rich man, the great house "like a palace," and the finding of their hearts' desire. Building for them in fact a palace of dreams, as brittle as the glass palace at Sydenham.

The weeks sped by until in the beginning of September

Blanche wrote to tell Tabbie that she had dragged Hubert away for a few days' rest and that they were staying with friends in Norwich.

"He will not consent to a stay of more than a few days," she wrote. *"And I am glad that our friend is not another physician as we understand from him that Norwich has had the prevailing plague very badly. But I hope we may come and see you while we are here. Hubert is more tired than he will admit and a day in the country will do him good."*

William said he would be delighted to see the Ashleys and a day was fixed for them to come. It happened to be a lovely warm late summer's day, and it was to be remembered by the young Hippenstalls as almost the best of their visit.

The Ashleys arrived early on the little train from Norwich: Tabbie thought they both looked tired and paler than when she had seen them last, but it might have been only in contrast to William's face sun-burned from his days in the fields where his men were getting in the last of the harvest. Both brother and sister were in good spirits however and entered into the children's games with enthusiasm running races and playing catch-as-catch-can until William suggested that as they had exhausted their guests they might take them indoors for a little light refreshment.

His housekeeper had served a cold collation in the large old-fashioned dining-room and afterwards, while the children made one of their explorations of the woods accompanied by the youngest and his nursemaid, William paced the lawn with Hubert discussing the possibility of the recent epidemic being connected with bad sanitation and water supplies, while the ladies sat in the shade of an old cedar talking of lighter things. "Some of our Norfolk towns are taking it seriously enough to have their sewers and water pipes closely examined," he said.

"And yet one cannot say definitely that drainage or bad water is the direct cause of it. Crowded living conditions could be equally culpable, or the fact that every city gutter is an open sewer in itself." The doctor fell silent, thinking about the one thing that was worrying him and others of his profession: how was the fever passed on? It was not infectious and it was not contagious, and yet it was handed from one to another. He went on as if thinking aloud, "If only some form of public privies could be introduced I believe it might reduce the risk of infection."

"I thought this had been suggested and it was decided that such places would only spread disease?"

"Yet would it spread it more than the gutters? Supposing cholera is spread through the excrement—as some believe—what better breeding grounds could there be than the gutters? You know yourself how people relieve themselves there—or else by the walls—and neither wall nor pavement is washed down with any frequency. More often than not it is left to the rain to cleanse our cities from their filth." He dropped a hand on his friend's shoulder. "Oh, William, I suppose the day will come when the human animal is a cleaner one, but there are times when I despair of him, and in the meantime thousands of lives go on being lost. But that is enough. Let us talk of lighter things."

William asked if Miss Fulgrove was still in Kensington.

"Oh no. She and Mrs. Gaywood fled to Brighton weeks ago."

"And Jarrett? How has he been behaving during the epidemic?"

"Remarkably well. Much as I dislike the fellow I have to give credit where it is due. He sent his mother to her sister in Leamington Spa, and he has been devoting all his time to the Rookery. I understand that the little maid was sent home on board wages, and he has his meals with Miss Knagg and the acidulated lady who gives her a home in Kensington. I am told she is her aunt." He gave a somewhat wry smile. "In fact, if Jarrett had been as ready to apply stoups as he was to hand out tracts, I should have found him invaluable. And in the meantime I cannot speak too highly of the excellent Miss Knagg, who has worked with us in a way that is beyond praise. She is a most worthy woman and I am sorry that he does not appear to appreciate her devotion. But perhaps it is as well." His eyes dwelt for a moment on Tabbie, and he said with anoher swift change of subject: "You have a nice place here, William. You will have to get married and produce a family as large as Sophy's. The house cries out for it."

William laughed and replied in an equally light vein and then the children were back, with blackberry stained faces and stories about a red squirrel that they had seen gathering nuts.

In the evening they gathered round the piano in the shadowed drawing-room to sing ballads while Tabbie played accompaniments for them all, and as he watched the candlelight shining on her bright hair and the eager faces of the older children, bronzed with summer sunshine, as they sang "Bonnie Dundee" and "My love she's but a lassie yet" Hubert wondered how Arnold could have had the strength of will to refuse the living only five miles away.

He thought it must be fatigue that was making him

weak enough to envy Arnold and to think of him with
anger, because as he had told William, they had worked
together in the Rookery as a team, and there had been
many moments when he had respected the young man.
But now that he had seen her again, he knew beyond all
doubt how deeply he was in love with Tabbie, and it did
not make it easy to join in the light-hearted songs round
the piano. His eyes were only for Tabbie, his thoughts
for her alone.

Sophy's youngest had been in bed for an hour or more
when the older children went out to play a last game of
catch before darkness fell and their mamma sent them off
to bed too. William took Blanche off to ask her advice
about his garden: the awe-inspiring Miss Ashley had a
look of fatigue that made her seem younger and less
alarming that evening, and he found himself calling her
Blanche easily, as Tabbie had done, and he did not mention drains or cess-pools once.

Did she think that nectarines would do well on that
north wall? They grew well in Westway but he was not
sure of the aspect. And did she know the name of the
rose over the porch, that his gardener called the Old
Glory? He picked the last one for her and was oddly
pleased when she tucked it into her belt.

He was thinking of sending for some Cochin hens, he
told her. Tabbie said that she kept Dorkings at St. Ursula's
for the sake of having fresh eggs for the patients. Were
Dorkings better layers than Cochins did she think? Dart-
ing from one thing to another and always shyly conscious
of the rose in her belt.

Dear William, Tabbie thought, strolling along behind
them with Hubert. The games with the children that
morning, and in fact the whole lovely day, had broken

down a lot of barriers of shyness and reserve where William was concerned. She wondered if her cousin was discovering that the 'dedicated woman' beside him could be capable of a great deal of human understanding beneath her rather austere manner.

She walked on beside Hubert amused but saying little, and scarcely noticing that he was very silent too, until suddenly she heard a nightingale down in the copse that William called rather grandly his "woods."

"Listen, Hubert!" She put her hand quickly on the doctor's arm, scarcely realising perhaps that for her too the barriers of reserve had come down that day. "Let us be still a moment. I'm sure I heard a nightingale down in those trees."

It was nearly dark. Ahead of them Blanche's light dress vanished round a clump of bushes on the way back to the house, and Hubert stood for a moment with his eyes on Tabbie's face, only conscious of her nearness and the hand on his arm. It was very quiet, in fact almost breathlessly still, and into the silence the bird's song suddenly broke in a silvery cadence of sound. To have Tabbie as close as this, with her smiling face turned towards him, her hand touching him, was almost more than he could stand.

He said abruptly, "I think we had better join the others, Tabbie, because if we don't, with that moon swinging up over those trees and that damned bird breaking my heart, I shall make love to you. And that would not be at all the thing."

The words were sharply, almost roughly spoken, the tone of his voice harsh and ironical, daring her to believe him, inviting her to laugh at him with himself, and then he turned and walked away towards the house, leaving her to follow, near to laughter and yet even nearer to tears.

That night she did not sleep very well. The song of the nightingale persisted down in William's woods, long after he had driven Hubert and his sister to the station to catch the last train back to Norwich, and it was, as Hubert had said, a song to break your heart.

William, coming into the house as his groom took the horse and trap to the stables, found Sophy still up. She was clearing the children's toys and books from the floor and chairs where they had been left, and as he came in she had just gathered up a small pile of brass framed photographs from the table in the window and was looking through them with a slightly puzzled air.

"Oh, William," she said, "I suppose you have not seen that photograph of Tabbie with Baby on her lap that was taken by that photographer on the beach at Yarmouth?"

"Is it not among those in your hand? And you should stop calling my namesake Baby, Sophy. He is getting too old for it."

"I daresay he is." Sophy spoke absently, her mind on the missing photograph. "I wonder where it could be?"

"I expect it has got in with the children's toys."

"Yes, I expect that is where it is. I will ask them if they have it in the morning." Sophy lighted her candle and went off to bed. But she did not ask her children in the morning if they had seen Tabbie's photograph, because in the middle of the night she woke up in the big double bed missing Sam and counting up the days to when she would be home again in Camberwell, and from that her thoughts went back to the day before and Tabbie's missing photograph. She tried to think when she had seen it last and then she suddenly remembered that it had been in the hands of Hubert Ashley, as he examined it in the light of the window.

"So that is where it has gone!" she told herself ruefully and she sighed. "I wish she were not engaged to that horrible Jarrett. I wish she would break her engagement to him . . . But having given her word she will never do that, and when he sees fit she will marry him and he will make her miserable for the rest of her life. My poor, poor Tab."

CHAPTER
9

By the end of September the cholera had subsided nearly everywhere and Sophy took her family back to Camberwell, while Tabbie returned to Kensington, to listen to her aunt's complaints about Cecily and the way she spoilt her children, and about Addy's nurse, who had quarrelled with the cook.

In due course Tabbie went back to the mending of the linen at St. Ursula's, missing the freedom of the countryside and William's happy-go-lucky way of life, and the smiling, fresh-faced country maids, so different from her aunt's superior London servants.

When she met Dr. Ashley again his manner towards her was the same as it had ever been—gravely polite and distantly friendly, and he called her "Miss Tabbie" once more as he had always addressed her in the past as Blanche's friend. Remembering that electric moment in the Norfolk garden she came to the conclusion that he had been joking, and that he had never intended her to take him seriously. Under such circumstances it seemed odd that she should feel as if a barrier had been erected between them: she thought it must be her imagination alone that had put it there, and yet she found she could not take one step towards breaking it down.

The first day of October was a day of national rejoicing, because of the news of a great victory having been won by the Anglo-French army before Sevastopol. The despatch added that it would only be a matter of hours before the city fell.

To celebrate the occasion Hubert took his sister to the Italian opera in Covent Garden, and they were returning from the performance when she suddenly gave a startled exclamation.

"Hubert," she cried, "tell Brenchley to stop. I am almost certain I saw a man lying in the gutter near the street lamp. He looked as if he were unconscious."

"Cholera," said the doctor laconically. "Or drunk." He told the coachman to stop, however, and getting out of the carriage he walked back a few yards and sure enough there was a huddled figure lying in the gutter beyond the lamp.

The man was not a victim of the cholera, however, and neither was he drunk. A deep gash oozing blood in his head and a slashed pocket in his coat showed that he had been set upon and robbed. As Hubert knelt beside him and felt his heart he opened his eyes with a faint groan.

"Damned fellows took me unawares," he muttered. "I put up a fight but there were too many of them. They got my wallet."

"Was there much money in it?"

"Not a great deal. Perhaps the best part of a hundred pounds in bank notes. Not more."

Hubert looked at the victim of the attack with greater interest. His clothes and speech were those of the well-to-do and the carelessness with which he spoke of the best part of a hundred pounds as being not much to lose, appeared to place him in a class that had always taken money for granted. He said gently, "You are lucky not to have been garotted."

"I daresay I am." The eyes that had been regarding him alertly now showed a tendency to close. "I will receive your congratulations later if I may. At the moment I am afraid I shall have to trouble you to fetch help. I cannot move of my own volition and I do not wish to spend the night in the gutter."

Hubert examined the cut as well as he could in the light from the gas-lamp. "How did you come to be here?" he asked.

"I had the notion that I'd like to visit a tavern in Maiden Lane—one I used to frequent with my cronies in my young days. But the faces I knew had all gone and it is not very convivial to sit drinking by one's self, and so I started to walk back to Cavendish Square. I daresay the ruffians followed me, attracted by the few sovereigns I'd spent with the landlord—not for his stout or for his brandy, which were both execrable—but for old times' sake."

"If you are bound for Cavendish Square, I have my carriage here and though my sister is with me, she will not faint at the sight of blood. I will bind up your head as best I can, and then my groom will help me get you into the carriage and I will take you home. I would like to see that cut properly washed and dressed before I leave you."

The sharp eyes opened again. "You speak like a sawbones," the man said.

"I am a physician, sir."

"Then I am extremely grateful to you. If your groom will give me an arm I daresay I can get as far as the carriage."

The carriage was backed to where he lay and the doctor having fashioned a make-shift bandage out of a pad made from the gentleman's handkerchief with his own scarf tied about it, lifted him into the carriage by taking him under the arms while the groom took his feet.

They propped him up on the seat while Blanche sat opposite and the doctor beside him to keep an arm about him and thus stop him from rolling off and on to the floor.

The house in Cavendish Square to which they were directed was a large mansion, but except for the lantern hanging over the steps it might have been untenanted. The windows were shuttered and fastened, and even in the dim light shed by the lamps in the square it had a neglected look, the paint shabby, some of the area railings missing.

Hubert sent the groom up the steps to pull the bell and the door was immediately answered by a man-servant who came hurrying to his master.

"Ah, there you are, Bates," said the gentleman. "I've been attacked by some ruffians who gave me a gash in my head. Fortunately this gentleman found me and brought me home."

"Oh, my Gawd!" The man Bates came up to the carriage. "I told your lordship not to go alone. I said it wasn't safe."

"Nonsense. Of course it was safe. And my skull is remarkably thick, as you know." The victim of the attack stirred himself, declaring he was able to get out of the carriage without assistance, but he would have fallen had not his man been there to take his weight.

With Hubert's assistance he got him upstairs to a large bedroom on the first floor, and the housekeeper sent the few servants there were in the house flying off for basins and hot water and towels.

The bedroom looked as neglected and unused as the outside of the house: the carpet was threadbare, the discoloured walls covered with old-fashioned pictures, but a cheerful fire was burning on the hearth and more candles were brought. Bates got his master into bed and Hubert stayed to examine him, dress his head and his bruises properly and told him to stay where he was for the next few days.

His lordship shot him an amused glance from under his heavy lids. In the candle-light his eyes were deeply, brilliantly blue. "I am not accustomed to being ordered about by my medical men," he said.

"Nevertheless you will obey my orders," said Hubert firmly.

"As you have been so devilishly obliging there is nothing else I can do I suppose," said his patient.

"I shall call on you tomorrow to be on the safe side," Hubert told him and the other laughed.

"Are you married?" he asked.

"No."

"I thought you were not. You have not the air of a married man. How have you managed to avoid the ladies then? I should guess you to be in your late thirties and you have a tolerable amount of good looks."

"Thank you. I am thirty-five." Hubert smiled ironically. "I daresay I have not found the right lady yet. The older ones are man-eaters and the younger ones are gigglers. Neither appeal to me."

"A medical man must find it hard to discover a piece of femininity that he is able to admire," agreed his patient, echoing William's opinion. "A lady cannot look her best whatever her age when she is suffering from a stomach-ache."

Hubert laughed and sent Bates downstairs for the small black bag that he always carried with him in his carriage, and administered an opiate before he left. He then left his name and address with the man and gave instructions that he was to send for him at once if he were uneasy about his master before he came on the following day, and then he went back to his carriage and was driven home.

"Scarcely such an enjoyable night as I had planned for you I'm afraid, my dear," he said as he joined his sister.

"Poor man, he had a horrid wound," Blanche said. "How old should you say he was? In the light as you carried him into the house I thought his hair was white."

"Rather fair, I think, going white. His face was not that of an old man, nor his body. I would say he was barely fifty years of age."

"Did you discover his name?"

"Yes. He is the Earl of Colleston."

"The Earl of Colleston." Blanche repeated the title thoughtfully. "I think I remember meeting his heir once—but he was a man of at least sixty, with children and grand-children. He was the Honourable Somebody Satterthwaite."

"This man's uncle I expect. Lord Colleston is not married and in fact his housekeeper told me that he seldom moves from his estates in Westmorland. He was simply on a visit to London. He plans to sell some property here."

"Was he seriously hurt?"

"Nothing that a few days in bed will not cure. I shall see him once more—I have a patient to see in Wimpole Street—but I shall not send in a bill and I do not suppose that after tomorrow I shall ever set eyes on him again."

Blanche said nothing. The charm of the man, in spite of his injury, had touched her, and she wished, not for the first time, that she could have a nearer contact with her brother's patients. But except for the rich snobs like the Sackroyds, and well-to-do spinsters of her own age, like Miss Fulgrove, who pursued her because through her they might lay hands on her brother, she was never invited to their houses.

It was about a week later that something happened that was to mark a turning point in Tabbie's life.

She was in the linen room at St. Ursula's busy cutting some sheeting into bed lengths when one of the nurses knocked at the door.

"I beg your pardon, Miss Sackroyd," she said. "Is Miss Ashley not here today? I looked in her office but there is nobody there and I cannot find her in the wards."

"Miss Ashley has a bad cold and her brother would not let her come," Tabbie said. "Is there anything I can do in her absence?"

"Well, it was Miss Ashley I wanted." The woman looked worried. "The fact is, Miss, it's that old Mrs. Styles being obstreperous, and I can't do nothing with her."

"Is that the old lady in Number Three?" asked Tabbie. There was an old lady in that room who was always causing trouble.

"Oh no, Miss. Mrs. Styles isn't a lady—leastways not what I would call a lady. Miss Ashley allowed her to have a bed in a room at the top of the 'ouse because she was an old servant of a friend of hers, but she has been nothing but a nuisance ever since she came, always asking for Miss Ashley to be with her, and you know, Miss, how busy she is. She 'asn't the time to sit 'olding an old woman's 'and hours at a time."

"Is Mrs. Morrish about?" asked Tabbie, not quite seeing what she could do under the circumstances.

"Mrs. Morrish is downstairs in the kitchen getting the dinner trays ready for the patients, and so I locked Mrs. Styles into her room while I came to see if I could find Miss Ashley."

"But why does she want Miss Ashley? Apart from having her hand held, I mean—poor old dear."

"Poor old nothing, Miss." The woman looked indignant. "It isn't Miss Ashley as she wants really—it's you. Miss Sackroyd is what she keeps asking for and that's why I come to find Miss Ashley seeing as you ain't allowed in the wards, not on no account. Them's Mrs. Morrish's orders, Miss."

"I see." Tabbie frowned, perplexed, "Well, as Miss Ashley isn't here and Mrs. Morrish is busy downstairs, perhaps I had better come and see if I can persuade Mrs. Styles to be quiet. She may have been one of my uncle's servants and that is why she knows my name." She put down her scissors and took off her thimble and slipped it into her pocket. Silver thimbles had a habit of disappearing sometimes in the linen room.

"I told her you wasn't allowed in the wards," the nurse continued, looking relieved, however, as Tabbie followed her up the stairs. "I said I'd get into trouble if I fetched you to 'er, but nothing will make 'er listen. I'm afraid she may get out of bed and fall like and break 'er leg. She's not fit to stand by 'erself, but she's that obstinate and scarcely knows what she's a doing of. But there seems like there's something on 'er mind, and she won't tell me of it."

They climbed to the top floor under the roof, and as they reached the landing the nurse stopped to fit the key into a door, saying that she did not know what Miss Ashley would say to the liberty she'd taken, not to say Mrs. Morrish neither. "But we 'ave no cholera cases 'ere and never 'ave 'ad none," she added.

"You have been lucky," Tabbie said encouragingly. "And I am glad I was here to help you with this old lady."

The nurse opened the door into a small attic room where an old woman was lying alone. Her bed had been moved into a patch of sunlight, though the room was warm enough with the September sun on the roof, and there were flowers in a vase on the table by her bed, and dimity curtains at the windows. She looked very old and frail, with her thin white hair lying like a cobweb over her pillow.

Tabbie went forward and sat down beside the bed. "You wanted to speak to me?" she said gently but distinctly.

The old eyes opened without recognition. "Miss Ashley?" Mrs. Styles said in a faint voice.

"Miss Ashley is not here today. She is not well. So I have come instead. I am Miss Sackroyd."

The effect of the name on the patient was extraordinary. Her eyes opened wide and studied her face eagerly, and then as the door closed behind the nurse the old woman said in a hurried voice, "You are the Miss Sackroyd that Miss Ashley told me of—Miss Tabitha Sackroyd, that is Sir Joseph Sackroyd's niece?"

"Yes." Tabbie's puzzlement grew. "What did you want to tell me?"

"Something I promised not to tell, but it must be told all the same." She was labouring now for breath. "I was nurse to a Miss Tabbie Sackroyd years ago." Her voice sank until it was scarcely audible. "She was Sir Joseph's sister—his only sister."

"She was my mother. My father was drowned in a rowing boat off the coast of Cornwall when I was a baby and when my mother died soon afterwards Sir Joseph brought me up as his own daughter." Tabbie stopped suddenly: the old eyes were regarding her with disconcerting shrewdness, and in spite of her weakness the old woman chuckled. It was a queerly ghostly sound, as if somebody was laughing from a distant age.

"So that was the story they put about?" she said. "Well, it was to be expected I suppose."

"What do you mean?" Tabbie was suddenly frightened of what the old creature was going to say: she wanted to run out of the room before she could hear it and yet at the same time she felt unable to move.

"Sir Joseph's sister—your mamma, my dearie—fell in love with a rascal," said Mrs. Styles, speaking with difficulty but with great clarity. "Sir Joseph was furious—he wanted her to marry a friend of his—a vulgar brute with a great deal of money. Treated her most cruel he did, because she wouldn't look at him, and so at last she ran away with her young gentleman. Sir Joseph went after them but he didn't find them for some time, and when he caught up with them he took her away. Used to having his own way was Sir Joseph and your poor little mamma was terrified of him. She'd been with her young gentleman for sometime then, however, and that was why I suppose Sir Joseph had to invent the drowning of your papa at sea, because you had no name but your mamma's. I was with her in the cottage in Cornwall and I nursed her when you was born to her there, and when she died and Sir Joseph came and took you away with him to London he paid me off and told me to hold my tongue. Nobody was to know what happened, and I wasn't to say a word to nobody, not never. So I've held my tongue, all these years. Paid me good money, he did, and I haven't said a word. Not until now. But I loved my Miss Tabbie and I couldn't meet my Maker if I didn't tell her daughter what I know. It needn't have been no shame to her you see, dearie, because that young gentleman, rascal as he was, would have married her—I lay a guinea he would, but it was the way Sir Joseph did it that broke her heart. She did not want to live after you was born, my poor pretty dear. It wasn't right for her brother to behave as he did—wicked and cruel he was to her, not letting her marry the young gentleman in the first place."

"Have you told Miss Ashley about this?" Tabbie felt so bewildered that she scarcely knew what she said.

"No, dearie, I've told nobody but you. It was when Miss Ashley said she had a Miss Tabbie Sackroyd working in the linen room and that you was Sir Joseph's niece that I knew you must be that baby in Cornwall. You don't blame me, do you, love? It is right that you should know, isn't it?"

"Yes. You were right to tell me—I am glad to know." Or perhaps she would be glad when she recovered from this profound sense of shock. "Who was my father? Can you tell me his name?"

"I don't remember. It was a long name—one what was difficult to stay in your mind like. I know he was a young swell with no money. His fambly had thrown him off, Sir Joseph said. Your mamma never said nothing about him during those months when we was waiting in Cornwall for you to come into the world, and when I spoke of him once she rounded on me and said I was never to mention him to her again. But if ever I saw a young lady what was broken-hearted my Miss Tabbie was that one." Her eyes closed again and after a moment she said, "Give me your hand, my dearie, if you will be so kind."

Tabbie put her hand into the rough one on the coverlet and felt the fingers close gently, almost like the touch of a feather, on hers. She was still sitting there when the nurse came back with a wrathful head nurse stalking ahead.

"The very idea!" exclaimed Mrs. Morrish angrily. "Letting Miss Sackroyd come into the wards. Miss Ashley will be very angry when she hears about this, and hear about it she will, I promise you."

"Hush!" Tabbie's gentle voice silenced the angry nurse. "I was very glad to be of use, and I think the old lady is asleep now." She slipped her hand out of the featherlike clasp. "I will come and see her again tomorrow. I am sure Miss Ashley will not mind."

But she did not see Mrs. Styles again because the old woman died that night, taking her secret and Tabbie's with her. Blanche was not well enough to come back to the hospital the next day, and when Tabbie heard of the old woman's death she asked Mrs. Morrish to say nothing of her visit to Mrs. Styles when Miss Ashley did return. She felt that the less people knew about it the better: it had to be kept even from good friends like Blanche.

CHAPTER
10

Tabbie said nothing about the little episode to her uncle or aunt: she felt it to be entirely her own problem, and fortunately for her they were not likely to notice any undue unresponsiveness on her part as October was not half way through before the news came that the battle of Alma that had been claimed as such a victory, had been followed by the most disastrous losses for the British troops. Nearly one hundred officers and more than two thousand men had either been killed or wounded, and Sevastopol had not fallen and showed no sign of doing so either.

"If the old Duke were alive this would never have happened," Sir Joseph kept saying, and while he and his lady discussed the prospect of Harry taking part in the fighting after so many casualties, Tabbie thought over the story that Mrs. Styles had told her and when the shock began to wear off a little she realised that whoever else need not know about it there was one who had the right to know and much as she might shrink from it, it was her duty to tell him.

One afternoon therefore she took the little maid Jenny that Mrs. Jarrett so much disliked and walked down to her house and asked if she might speak to Arnold.

He happened to be at home and he took her into the cupboard-like study where he had been attempting to compose a sermon on the pride of riches. "Well, Tabbie, what is it?" he asked impatiently.

"I've heard something recently about my mother that has shocked and—frightened me," she said, appealing for his help, his understanding and his love.

"Indeed?" His tone chilled her. "What is that?"

She told him falteringly the story that Mrs. Styles had told her before she died, and he said nothing until she had finished: the help and understanding and love that she had counted on, however, did not seem to be there.

He sat with clouds gathering on his brow as if she were confessing to her own sin instead of her mother's and when she had done he pushed aside his sermon and stared away from her out of the little window to the street outside. Two girls were going down the street crying fresh watercresses, though from the look of the wilted bunches in their baskets it was doubtful if any river in England could have grown them in that condition. As their voices died away he said abruptly:

"Of course, unpleasant as gossip of this nature is, it has not come as any surprise to me, and I do not suppose it would surprise any of your uncle's friends either. Garrulous old women, as this Mrs. Styles appears to have been, would not stop at telling one person such a spicy piece of gossip. I do not doubt that she has told many others in her time. Certainly nobody in Kensington ever believed

the story of the naval officer and the rowing boat. As
Miss Fulgrove remarked once to Mamma it was just a polite excuse for your existence."

"Miss Fulgrove?" A sense of nightmare was attacking
Tabbie. "Did you say that Miss Fulgrove discussed my affairs with Mrs. Jarrett?"

"Is there any reason why she should not?"

"No—I suppose not." Only good taste, which Miss
Fulgrove did not possess.

"Selina Fulgrove is a woman of the world, my dear,
and she put her finger on the weak spot in your story at
once. If there ever had been a naval officer, she asked,
where were his relatives? Did they all go down with him
in the rowing boat? She can be very amusing at times. As
she said the story of the father drowned at sea was one of
the oldest in the world, but she did not blame Sir Joseph
for having taken the opportunity when it arose to win
respectability for his niece."

"Repectability? And for me?" Tabbie stared. "What
did she mean?"

"Why, that to be the wife of a clergyman—to be *my*
wife, Tabbie—would give you a position that you would
not be likely to attain in any other way. That is why of
course your uncle has never mentioned your parentage to
me, and I am sure that most of your mother's family,
fully aware that she was not married and that you are in
fact her illegitimate daughter and the skeleton in the
family cupboard, must have been every bit as relieved as
Sir Joseph when we became engaged."

"I understand." She got up: her face was very white
but she was strangely composed. "Thank you for explain-
ing everything to me so fully, Arnold. I will call my maid

now and go home. Please make my excuses to Mrs. Jarrett."

"I will walk with you. I have a visit to make in that direction and it is no good trying to return to my sermon after this interruption."

"Thank you. In that case I will tell Jenny she may go home without waiting any longer."

Jenny was called up from the basement and departed happily, glad to be done with Mrs. Jarrett's dark little kitchen with its chocolate paint, its smoky ceiling, and its black beetles.

Arnold fetched his hat and walked up the High Street with Tabbie, glancing at her uneasily from time to time and wondering if he had said too much. But Miss Fulgrove's words to his mother had been festering in his mind for a long time, and it was as well that his betrothed should know the truth. She could no longer call him to account for refusing livings that did not suit him without consulting her. Under the circumstances she could not claim the right to be consulted: the prospect of being his wife was a piece of luck that she had never appeared to appreciate properly, but after this no doubt she would know better.

Tabbie said no more until they were nearly home and then feeling that she could not face her uncle's cold and loveless house without having done what she came to do, she asked Arnold to take a turn in the Gardens with her, adding, "I will only keep you from your parishioners for a few minutes."

They entered the Gardens and found a secluded seat screened by laurels, and as they sat down Tabbie said quietly:

"First I must apologise for having misled you, but it

was unwittingly done on my part. Your mother told me some time ago that you had expected a great deal more than my five hundred pounds when you became engaged to me. You considered that my uncle was a rich enough man to treat me as generously as he treated his daughters. But as you pointed out just now, I am not his daughter, but the skeleton in his family's cupboard, and everybody knew it. I can only ask you to believe that had I known it when you asked me to marry you I would not have accepted you. Fortunately there is still time for that to be remedied."

She felt in the pocket of her skirt and took something from it and handed it to him, dropping it into his hand.

"Here is your ring, Arnold. Although marriage with you would give me the—'respectability' I think was Miss Fulgrove's word—that I lack, I could not marry any man for that reason alone. The material advantages of being your wife did not occur to me until now: I fancied it to be an engagement of affection on both sides. It seems I was mistaken. I have no more to say—except goodbye—and God bless you."

Arnold found himself completely taken in. Ever since his mother had repeated her conversation with Miss Fulgrove he had fancied himself to be the injured party, the one who was to be thanked for having stooped to Sir Joseph's poor little niece. And now in some way that he failed to understand the tables appeared to have been turned, and the dignity with which she dismissed him put him completely in the wrong. He flushed angrily as he protested:

"Do you think you are wise to act in this precipitate fashion? I would advise you to think it over, Tabbie, before you cause further scandal with a broken engagement.

I do not suppose you will ever have another proposal of marriage, with the whole of Kensington aware of your history."

"I do not suppose so either." She would not let him see how deeply he hurt her. "But there may be compensations in spinsterhood unknown to us both. And now do not let us prolong this unhappy interview any longer. Please go."

"But I cannot leave you alone in the Gardens like this. What will people think? You have dismissed your maid."

"With my parentage I can scarcely afford to care what people think about me, nor can I expect to be treated as a lady. Goodbye, Mr. Jarrett."

The feeling that he had behaved badly increased and it deepened his anger. "Very well, I am sure I am the last to stay where I am not wanted. Goodbye, Miss Sackroyd." He dropped the ring into his pocket, lifted his hat, and walked hastily away.

She looked after him for a few minutes, saying farewell to five years of her life, while all the small slights and odd little snubs endured by her in the past suddenly became clear: Louisa's embarrassment when she had let slip that she had told Mrs. Rawlings she did not know who Tabbie's father was had showed repercussions that did not stop with the Sackroyds. It spread to their friends and beyond, to connections by marriage. All these things, coming to her so harshly and so cruelly, took the courage from her heart and the fire from her spirit. She bent her head in her hands and allowed herself the luxury of tears.

It was thus that Hubert Ashley saw her a few minutes later as he walked home across the park.

"Why, it's Tabbie—and alone! My dear, what is the matter?" In a couple of strides he was beside her, the barrier between them gone. It was the old Hubert, the friend of the day at Sydenham, the Hubert of the Norfolk visit, who was there to console her, and somehow it did not matter that he found her at a disadvantage and in tears.

"It is nothing." She struggled to produce a smile for him but the effort was too much and although she tried to brush them away the tears still welled up and dropped like diamonds on her shawl. He longed to take her in his arms to comfort her, but instead he put his arm along the back of the seat and waited, and presently she pulled herself together and told him the story she had heard from Mrs. Styles and how Arnold had confirmed it, saying it was common knowledge.

"Common to everyone it seems, but me," she went on forlornly after a despairing glance at his face had shown her that it was not news to him either. "I never dreamed that what I had been told about my father was not true. When you are naturally truthful yourself you do not think that your nearest relatives will bring you up in the shadow of a lie. I wish Uncle had told me the truth. It would have been easier to bear than to have discovered it like this." She wiped her eyes and put her handkerchief away. "I have broken my engagement with Arnold Jarrett—although he assured me that I would not have another proposal of marriage and I daresay he is right. But when he walked away just now I felt for the moment that I could have died—not for what he had said, but for what he did not say. Poor Arnold."

Hubert experienced a strong desire to hurry after poor Arnold and knock him down. His frown deepened as he said gently, "Tabbie, my dear, whatever people may say I am sure you have always been regarded with real affection by every member of your uncle's family. It has never made any difference to them—or to any of your real friends."

She sat silent and unconvinced, her mind going to her uncle's house—the house that Sophy had called a glass palace. And how apt the description was, for all Sophy's laughter.

The life within that house had always been as empty and as meaningless as life in a glass palace would be: there was no warmth in it, no heart, no real love. Only a brittle awareness of how its grandeur should impress the outside world. She wished she had not to go back to it: her whole being shrank from her aunt's anger when she heard of the broken engagement, but at this moment not even the thought of that anger could outweigh the feeling of shame that was with her still, because she alone of that household had not known the truth of her mother's story.

And then Hubert said, choosing his words with care, "You know I have many patients in London as well as here in Kensington, and among them I can number some from old and aristocratic families. You would be surprised if you knew how many members of those families would find it hard to tell with any degree of certainty who their fathers were. The world gossips and guesses, but they carry their heads high and dare their friends to conjecture as they will. It may be poor comfort at the moment, little Tabbie, but you are in good company."

This time she managed to return his encouraging smile, if somewhat shakily.

"Thank you," she said. "Dear Hubert—I will remember that."

Especially would she remember it when she caught the looks of condescending pity between her aunt's friends, and although it must all return to her from time to time with a sense of agonised shame, the kindness of this good friend would help her.

"Then," he said, watching her sad face in half-smiling concern, "let me take you home with me to Blanche. Her cold is almost gone and she is very impatient with me for not letting her put her nose outside the front door this afternoon. We will ask Mrs. Webb for one of her excellent plum cakes, and the quince jam that nobody makes quite as she does, and Blanche will send a note to your aunt telling her that you are spending the evening with us. That will give you time to find your feet again before you see your family."

"I would rather that Blanche did not know about Mrs. Styles," she said.

"She shall not know. We will tell her that your engagement is at an end and that you are feeling rather sad about it. Come, take my arm and let me take you to her."

She did not demur any more, and as she walked back with him to his house the warmth came back to her heart and the courage to her spirit, with which to meet the demands that must be made upon her in the weeks to come.

As for him, he would not have been human had not a wild hope raised its head in his heart, but it was neither the time nor the place in which to indulge such fancies. Five years had to be deleted first, and he did not know how long they would be remembered. It was plain to him that for her he was simply Blanche's kindly brother, and for that he felt he must be thankful.

CHAPTER
11

Arnold walked away rapidly from the Gardens, forgetting about his parish visit in the ferment of his thoughts, in which anger against Tabbie was uppermost. How dare she give him back his ring and dismiss him in such a fashion, when he had shown her such magnanimity? Had he said one word of wanting to be free of his engagement—one might almost say of his entanglement—with her?

He walked on, scarcely knowing where he was going, until he found himself in the High Street with Addison Road not far away. He would be certain of sympathy from Miss Fulgrove—he was sure she had never approved of his engagement to Tabbie in her heart. Had she not hinted from time to time that he was worthy of somebody in a very different class from Sir Joseph Sackroyd's penniless niece? Well, not penniless exactly, but what was five hundred pounds to a woman with Miss Fulgrove's wealth?

It was then that the staggering thought came to him

that he was now free to marry somebody else, and one moreover who had shown him continual kindness for months past. Selina had forgiven him long ago for his behaviour at Sydenham, and after her visitors had gone she had received him as kindly as before. In fact, since she had returned from Brighton she had referred to his conduct during the cholera epidemic as heroic.

The possibility of winning such a wealthy wife made his heart beat and his face flush. What a triumph it would be, and how he would be able to score off Tabbie and those vulgar Sackroyds who had snubbed him so unmercifully over the years.

As he dwelt on the encouragement that Selina had given him he might be forgiven for the conceit that made him believe she had meant something more. The ring in his pocket would not be good enough for her of course, but the shop where he had bought it might allow something on it if he purchased a finer one. His head now well in the clouds and with his spirits lifting every moment he hurried to Addison Road.

Miss Fulgrove's house was separated by a few feet from its neighbours: a tessellated path led through the forecourt from the iron gate to the porch, the front door being set back between the pillars that supported the porch roof. He pushed open the gate and walked briskly up the path to the front door and pulled the iron bell-handle. He heard the bell jangle in the basement kitchens and the page-boy's voice telling the butler that there was someone at the door. In a few minutes steps were heard crossing the hall floor within and the door opened and the elderly man-servant stood there.

Miss Fulgrove was at home, and as Arnold entered the house he thought with satisfaction that this was how things should be: one man-servant to open the door and to look after the wine cellar and the silver, a page-boy to run errands and female servants to wait on one and one's guests. No grinning footmen with powdered hair and padded calves inside their silk stockings should ever set foot inside his house.

He was shown into the drawing-room and was fortunate enough to find Miss Fulgrove alone there, busy with her needlework.

"Why, Mr. Jarrett!" she said warmly. "This is a pleasure. Mrs. Gaywood has only just this moment run upstairs to find me some of her Berlin wool. I have run out of purple, you see, and I cannot finish this rose without it."

He had no time to admire the needlework or to talk of Berlin wools: he must be quick if he were to say what he had come to say before Mrs. Gaywood returned.

He took Selina's hand in his and kissed it fervently, and then before the astonished lady had time to draw it away, he was down on his knees on the Brussels carpet, telling her that he was a free man, and asking her to reward his undying love by promising to be his wife.

To say that she was furious was putting it mildly. At any moment Julia would come in and see her and Mr. Jarrett in this ridiculous situation. She got quickly to her feet, dragged her hand away from his, and told him to get up at once and not be so absurd.

"You are engaged to be married!" she reminded him.

"No, dearest lady, I am not. Tabitha Sackroyd released me from our engagement this afternoon, to our mutual relief. It was wrong from the start and my affections were never involved. I am free." Still he could not see beyond his own ambitions. "Selina, you must not play with me.

It would be too cruel. Why, for weeks—nay for months—
you have encouraged me to hope. You cannot dash those
hopes to the ground now. But I know you will not."

"Mr. Jarrett, I can only think that you have been
drinking." Gone was the kindness and gone were the
smiles. Miss Fulgrove's fury was increased by the uneasy
feeling that there might be a grain of truth in what he had
said about her encouragement. To a man with Arnold
Jarrett's conceit it might indeed have seemed that she had
been encouraging him, when she had simply been indulg-
ing her own liking for telling him what he should or
should not do in the parish. She liked telling people what
they should or should not do, and they usually followed
her advice which was all to the good because it was sound
advice and pleased her as well as them. "When you are
more yourself," she went on cuttingly, "you will realise
that you are no more fitted to be my husband than I am
to be the wife of a penniless curate. I am extremely sorry
that you have so misconstrued my well-meant efforts at
helping you in your parochial problems, but I am
prepared to forget what you have said and conclude that
if, as you say, Miss Sackroyd has broken your engagement, you are too upset to know what you are doing. My
advice to you now is to find her as soon as possible and
put things right." She went to the bell and rang energetically for the man-servant to show him out. "Mr. Jarrett
has to go now," she said, and bowed in Arnold's direction
without looking at him. "Good afternoon, Mr. Jarrett."

Dazedly he returned to the street and made his way
back to his tiny study where the half-written sheets of his
sermon awaited him. He sat for a long time without writing a word, and indeed scarcely knowing where he was,
but he had the sense at last to realise that it was entirely

due to the whims of a spoilt rich woman and the overweening ambition she had raised in him, that he had looked on Tabbie with ever increasing contempt until today he had lost her. He knew too that he would be unable to take Selina's last piece of advice: the unforgiveable things he had said that afternoon made it impossible for him to seek out Tabbie and "put things right."

In the meantime Mrs. Gaywood came back with the purple wool to find her friend walking about her drawing-room like a caged lioness, her face flushed, her eyes sparkling with anger.

"Was that Mr. Jarrett who called?" asked Mrs. Gaywood innocently, having witnessed the young man's departure from her bedroom window. "He stayed a very short while."

"Not short enough for my comfort," said Selina. "You were right, Julia, and I give you leave to say that you told me so. This afternoon Tabitha Sackroyd gave him his *congé* and the—the little horror—came here hotfoot to propose to me. The impertinence of it!"

"If he has a big opinion of himself, my dear, you have only yourself to blame," said Mrs. Gaywood mildly and then she added with some curiosity, "If old Mr. Prince dies in the night, will you ask your brother to consider Mr. Jarrett for the living?"

"The last time I spoke to Walter about it," Selina said, "he told me that he felt it to be his duty to offer it to the old gentleman's son, who had been doing half the work of the parish for his father for the last twenty-five years."

Mrs. Gaywood thought that under those circumstances it was a pity her friend had dissuaded Arnold Jarrett from accepting other livings. He was an odious little man and she disliked him intensely, but with Tabbie for his wife she supposed he might have improved over the years. Selina said nothing and in fact she was so silent for the rest of the day that Mrs. Gaywood hoped she was ashamed of herself.

When the neighbourhood had recovered from the shock of Tabbie's broken engagement however, a further shock was in store for his friends, when Mr. Jarrett accepted a very poor living in Kent. Rumour had it that it was one that had been offered to him before and pity was felt for his mother until it was discovered that Miss Knagg had consented to accompany her son as his wife, to the undying fury of her bosom friend Miss Capp, who never spoke to her again.

Mrs. Jarrett was free to depart to Leamington and it was generally felt that Miss Knagg, being an eminently sensible woman with a nice little sum in the funds, would soon get the Kent village into shape and the vicarage habitable and even comfortable for her husband.

Sir Joseph liked to read the morning newspaper to Lady Sackroyd and Tabbie after breakfast, taking an almost sadistic pleasure in cutting its pages first with the paper knife with the greatest possible care. The paper was *The Times*, radical as it was, and Tabbie thought that he subscribed to it largely because its political views differed so widely from his own. He liked a one-sided argument and one with the absent editor of a newspaper was better than nothing.

Apart from becoming a little quieter and paler than before Tabbie had settled down with outward contentment to taking her old place as her aunt's companion in the household. She read aloud to Lady Sackroyd in the evenings, or played chess with her uncle—William had taught her to play when she was eight years old. Her broken engagement was never discussed and in fact it was a subject avoided by them all because there were more important things on their mind that autumn, and Sir Joseph and his contemporaries bewailed the fact that the old Duke was no longer there to direct the war.

"We shall never see another Wellington," he said. "He would not have had all this parleyvooing with the French. He would have told *them* what to do. But here is our General actually taking orders from a Frenchman!" Humiliation could go no deeper than that.

When he read the account of the hard-fought battle of Alma, however, he admitted that perhaps the French might turn out to be better allies than he had anticipated. "Though mind you," he added warningly, as if Tabbie or her aunt had had something to do with it, "they could have done nothing without us. It says here that our magnificent men went into battle in solid ranks as if they were parading in Hyde Park."

It was not until October 9th when Russell's despatches began to come through that it was discovered that those same magnificent men were being left to die in their hundreds because of the utter neglect and inefficiency of the British Army Medical Staff.

Not only was the hospital at Scutari completely inadequate for the reception of the thousands of cholera cases and the many wounded and dying men sent down from the battlefield, but there were not nearly enough nurses or dressers or surgeons or even dressings with which to treat their wounds.

Here, added Russell, to the mortification of Sir Joseph and those of his fellow countrymen who read his Radical newspaper that morning and suffered from dyspepsia for the rest of the day in consequence, the French had shown themselves to be vastly our superiors. Their medical arrangements were extremely good, their surgeons numerous, and they also had the help of their Sisters of Charity, who were excellent nurses.

Not for them a government so mean-minded as to cut the Army and its supplies to the bone in times of peace, leaving that Army with nothing behind it when war came upon the nation. Wellington's well-planned wagon trains of supplies had been thrown on the scrap-heap years ago, and according to Russell it had even been forgotten that old rags were necessary for the dressing of wounds.

On the day following this report Blanche called for Tabbie in the carriage rather earlier than usual and asked her if she would mind being left on her own in the linen room that morning, as she had to go and see somebody on urgent business. Tabbie was pleased to escape from her uncle's house, where Louisa had arrived from the country the night before in a great state of nervous terror about her beloved Harry, and Dr. Ashley had been called in to administer a soothing draught and to assure her that the officers' quarters in Scutari would be vastly different from those of the troops.

"Hampers of good food and champagne," he told her reassuringly. "That is all the medicine that Major Rawlings will need." And as hampers of good food and champagne had pursued Harry ever since he left England Louisa felt comforted enough to think that she might be able to return to Hampshire again and the petting of Harry's parents by the end of the week. But it had not prevented her from sharing Tabbie's bed and keeping her awake into the small hours.

At mid-day Blanche called for Tabbie to walk home with her—the carriage not being available—and as they went she told her what her urgent business had been. She had received a letter from Miss Nightingale that morning telling her that she was arranging to take a small band of nurses to the Crimea and she had asked if Blanche would furnish her with the names of any experienced women at St. Ursula's who would be prepared to go with her. Blanche had called on Miss Nightingale that morning to offer her own services. "Mrs. Webb will look after Hubert as well as if I were here," she said. "And Miss Nightingale knows that I am not a fine lady over nursing. I will scrub floors and empty bed-pans with the best of them."

"When does she expect to go?" asked Tabbie.

"In three days' time, on October the 17th. But she has to ask for her release from the Harley Street committee first, as I must from the committee of St. Ursula's. I do not think we shall be refused, mind you. Everybody is up in arms about these terrible conditions in Scutari." She hesitated. "I know you are, very young, Tabbie, but you have a good sensible head on your shoulders. I would like to put your name forward as lady superintendent in my place, while I am away. Do you think your uncle would consent to it?"

"I do not see why he should not," said Tabbie. Indeed, ever since her engagement had been broken off it had seemed as if her uncle and aunt were almost glad of any excuse to leave her at home when they went out, and to encourage her to go out to any friends who might invite her to their houses.

"And you would not feel it too much of an imposition?" pursued Blanche.

"As long as you will leave me Mrs. Morrish," said

Tabbie smiling. "If you were to take her with you to the Crimea I should be lost indeed."

"I should not dream of taking her from you," Blanche said.

Sir Joseph and his lady made no objection to Tabbie's new work at St. Ursula's: in fact although Lady Sackroyd appeared to think it extraordinary of Miss Ashley to wish to go out to the Crimea in order to nurse rough soldiers, she seemed almost relieved to think that Tabbie would be employed every day of the week at the hospital in her absence.

"I understand that Miss Ashley has her own room there and that she is chiefly employed on keeping the hospital accounts," she said. "You have always had a good head for figures—I know you can add up a great deal easier than Louisa or Addy—and as long as that head nurse is at St. Ursula's I see no objection to you working there."

"You don't mind being left alone now that Louisa is back in Hampshire?" Tabbie persisted. She felt she should be with her aunt for the best part of the day.

"Oh pray do not bother your head about me, my dear!" Lady Sackroyd spoke sharply. "My sisters have plenty of daughters who will be pleased to come and stay here for weeks at a time. I can always fill your place! My sister Helen's eldest, Fanny, will be delighted to come. A plain child, with rabbit's teeth, but very obliging. I am sure she will do very well."

It was not a kind speech, and not for the first time Tabbie felt that her aunt resented the breaking off of her engagement, although she had never troubled to hide her dislike for Arnold. She had implied more than once lately that he had been quite good enough for Tabbie, and that she had shown ingratitude to her uncle by being dependent on him still for her board and keep—and indeed, for promising to be so for the rest of her life. Tabbie began to wonder if her aunt had always resented her presence in the house, from the time that she had been brought there as a baby of three months old.

The following day they heard that Miss Nightingale's journey had been postponed for a week or two until she could gather forty nurses to take with her to the Crimea. It appeared that the Government had asked her to take charge of an official expedition. No female nurses had been allowed to nurse soldiers before, and it was thought that the male nurses there had so little experience of nursing the sick that they might lose many lives through sheer ignorance.

Miss Ashley was asked once more to appeal to the St. Ursula's nurses, and she sent for the head nurse that same morning and read out Miss Nightingale's requirements to her.

Listening with astonishment Tabbie could not believe that any nurse would be encouraged to volunteer her services under such conditions, and when she was alone with Blanche again she said so.

"Some of the rules seem so petty," she said. "They must not wear coloured ribbons or flowers for instance."

"But our Mrs. Webb will never engage a housemaid who wears ribbons or flowers," Blanche pointed out. "And I am sure Lady Sackroyd's housekeeper does the same. That is nothing unusual."

Tabbie said wistfully that she wished she could volunteer to go.

"You would not be strong enough," Blanche said firmly. "The work will be arduous and difficult, and you are inexperienced in nursing, even if you were not too young, my love. Miss Nightingale insists on older women because they will be less trouble. She will have enough on her hands without having to look after a number of young women." She smiled affectionately at the girl. "If we can get the committee's consent, you will be serving your countrymen and women just as well by working here at St. Ursula's in my place."

The list of requirements set out by Miss Nightingale might seem to be formidable, but they were dictated solely by common sense, as Blanche explained to Tabbie when they walked home together that afternoon after a disappointing response from the St. Ursula's nurses. Only one had volunteered to go, and she had not done so from any high sense of vocation, but simply because of the money, which was twice the amount that any nurse could earn in a hospital at home.

"That is why Miss Nightingale insists that each nurse who volunteers to accompany her must submit herself absolutely to her orders, and she had made very strict rules about misconduct with the troops and so forth. A nurse invalided home will have her expenses paid first class, but anyone sent home for bad behaviour will travel third class on salt rations."

"Have you seen the uniform that is being supplied?" asked Tabbie.

"I have, and I can assure you that it is hideous," said Blanche laughing. "I shall make a point of wearing it myself though. Hubert says that he does not think we shall be welcomed by the Army doctors, and that the prejudice of such men will be harder to defeat than the Russians. That is why Miss Nightingale sets her face against ribbons and flowers and so on. If the party of women she takes with her give the impression of being a party of motherly old bodies armed with umbrellas and carpet bags she will be more likely to succeed in her object—which is nursing the sick and wounded—than if she arrives with a party of drabs. Already she is finding it very difficult to discover the kind of women she needs, and one of the stumbling blocks is that she will have no drunkeness, she will allow none of them to go out without leave, and when they go out they will have to be accompanied by more than one other nurse, while they will have to wear the uniform at all times—for their own protection."

"When do you think you will go?"

"Miss Nightingale hopes to leave London on October 21st." Blanche gave Tabbie's arm a little squeeze. "I shall miss you, little Tabbie." And then Hubert's carraige overtook them to take Tabbie home before dropping Blanche.

During the days that followed the committee gave its consent for Sir Joseph Sackroyd's niece to take over Blanche's work at the hospital, Fanny of the rabbit's teeth arrived to take her place in Palace Gardens and every moment she could spare from mending the linen Tabbie spent in the little room that her friend used as an office, learning the procedure of paying the weekly bills, and how to keep accounts. She was taken round the hospital with the keys of the store cupboards and memorised the contents of each cupboard, and how groceries were ordered at wholesale prices. Then there was the house surgeon to meet and his dispensary to visit.

"Mr. Newton will help you as much as he can," Blanche promised her. "If there is any medicine you are suspicious about take it to him at once. Some of them are not labelled correctly. But Mrs. Morrish will be a tower of strength at all times."

There was no question now of Tabbie not being allowed in the wards. In her grey stuff gown with its white collar and cuffs, and her bright hair banded round her small head under a frilled cap, she might look young, but there was an air of dignity and gentle compassion in her that gave her authority.

"I don't know where Tabbie gets her way of managing others," Blanche told her brother one evening. "Certainly not from her uncle or aunt, who simply order things to be done as if their servants were automatons. She tells the nurses what she wants them to do in that gentle way of hers, and her voice is so firm and the smile that accompanies the order so sweet, and the word of thanks afterwards so quick in coming, that already they question nothing. I shall have no hesitation in leaving St. Ursula's in her hands." And then, as Hubert did not answer, she added, "Did you hear what I said, Hubert? About Tabbie I mean?"

"Oh," he said heavily, "yes, I heard."

"May I tell her tomorrow that you will be looking in on her once or twice in the week to see how she is getting on?"

"Certainly not."

"But—why not?"

"My dear Blanche, Newton is a good man and as perfectly capable of treating the patients at the hospital when you are not there as he is when you are there. It would be quite unpardonable on my part to interfere."

"But Tabbie . . ."

"Your Tabbie has grown up during the last few weeks. Have you not noticed it? She is a woman now and able to manage her own affairs." He got up and dropped his hand on her shoulder. "If you must go off to Scutari then you must, but do not try to manage St. Ursula's as well. Tabbie and Newton will do very well between them." And then saying that he had some letters to write he said good night and left her.

CHAPTER
12

Two evenings before Blanche was to leave for Scutari a servant came to see her in the drawing-room to say that a gentleman had called to see her and the doctor and would not give his name.

Hubert was out but Blanche told the man to show the gentleman upstairs, and a few minutes later the Earl of Colleston was shown into the room.

"Miss Ashley?" He took the hand she held out to him and then stared with some amazement at the dress she was wearing.

"I see you are admiring the uniform we nurses are to wear when we accompany Miss Nightingale to Scutari," she said laughing. "I tried it on tonight because I hoped to amuse my brother when he comes in. Is it not attractive?"

The dress was of plain black woollen material, with an unbleached linen apron and a scarf across the shoulders from left to right, embroidered with the words SCUTARI

HOSPITAL in red thread. Her slippers were of felt, so that they should not make any sound, she explained. "Fortunately," she added, "my maid has been clever enough to make the dress fit, because they are all in one size, and tall or short, fat or thin, we have to take what is given us."

His lordship listened with interest and then he remarked drily that Miss Nightingale was lucky to have ladies dedicated enough to consent to wear such atrocious garments.

Blanche only laughed, however, and apologised for her brother's absence, but added that he would be in very soon.

"No matter." He brushed it aside as of no consequence. "Before I left London I wished to settle with your brother for his attendance on me, but he refused to take any payment saying that he would have done the same for anyone. Now I do not like to be in the debt of a man who works as hard as he does and you will find downstairs a haunch of venison that my man Bates is introducing at this moment to your cook. I hope you will enjoy it."

"You are very kind. My brother is very fond of venison: he will find it a great treat." It was at this moment that Hubert returned and she went to the top of the stairs to meet him, letting him laugh at her dress before bringing him into the drawing-room to meet his ex-patient.

"As Blanche leaves London in two days' time," Hubert said, "and my experience of venison is that it must hang for some considerable time before it is fit to eat, can I not persuade you to taste it with me, in a week or two's time?"

His visitor shook his head. "I must decline the pleasure, Dr. Ashley, for I too will not be in London more than a few days. It seems from one's perusal of the newspapers that not only are we lamentably short of men out there in the Crimea, but if the reports on the Scutari Hospital are correct, we are likely to be rather more short in a very little while. My man and I, therefore, have travelled to London with the idea of taking the Queen's shilling."

"You are enlisting?" Dr. Ashley's eyes met the brilliant blue ones with a shock of surprise. "And in the ranks?"

"Why not? I am no better than any other man who enlists I suppose? I am told we are given six weeks training before we are sent abroad, and if they will supply me with a rifle that will not explode in my hand I will guarantee to pick off any Russian out there who happens to be within range."

Blanche asked him if he would not stay to dinner. "It will give me an excuse to change out of this hideous dress," she told him smiling. "And we would like to entertain you before the Army takes you."

"You give me no alternative," he said gallantly. "I will be pleased to stay."

Word was sent to the kitchen, much to the relief of Bates, who had been watching mouth-watering preparations going forward for the doctor's evening meal, and Blanche went away and exchanged the black wool dress for a golden-coloured velvet, more in keeping with the October evening. She came back to find the two men deep in conversation about the conduct of the war, which continued through the meal that followed in the mellow candle light of the dinner table.

When the two gentlemen joined her in the drawing-room later, however, she tried to introduce a lighter note by telling his lordship about Harry Rawlings and the hampers of good food and champagne.

"Our friends the Sackroyds are quite consoled now," she told him. "They can see their son-in-law being protected on all sides by Messrs. Fortnum and Mason and champagne. As he is in the Light Cavalry Brigade one does not anticipate any great danger for him though, as long as he can escape the cholera."

"Yes, the Light Brigade will not be selected for any spectacular campaigning I imagine." Their guest was frowning however. "Sackroyd," he repeated in a tone of some distaste. "That name is a familiar one to me. Are you speaking of Sir Joseph Sackroyd's family?"

"Yes. They live quite near us."

"I know that. I have seen the house."

Blanche was pleased that he should know their friends. "They are patients of my brother's," she told him, "as well as our personal friends."

"I am sorry." Lord Colleston was suddenly stiff and his voice had lost its warmth. "That they are your brother's patients and your friends, Miss Ashley."

"I cannot choose my patients, sir," the doctor protested. "It is they who choose me."

"I am sure of that, but I would not choose Sir Joseph Sackroyd as my friend."

"Why? What have you against him?" Hubert checked himself. "I beg your pardon. I should not have asked that."

"On the contrary. I do not object to telling you. The man is a murderer."

"A murderer?" Blanche was incredulous, and he turned on her sternly.

"You do not believe me, Miss Ashley? And yet I assure you that I am telling you the truth when I say that he killed my wife." This statement was followed by an

awkward little silence as Blanche and her brother tried to
assimilate it and then he asked in a constrained voice:
"Of what does his family consist?"

"He has two sons and two daughters." Blanche was
distressed. "I assure you, Lord Colleston, they are a very
nice family."

"I am sure they are." His voice was heavy with irony.

"And then there is their niece, Tabitha, who is a particular pet of mine," went on Blanche. "She helps me in the
linen room at our little hospital for sick ladies in Old
Brompton."

"I did not know that Sir Joseph had a brother. Surely
there could not be two Sackroyd monsters in the world?"

"You are determined to be unkind about our friends."
Blanche tried to win him out of his sombre mood. "Tabbie is Sir Joseph's sister's child. She died soon after Tabbie was born and he adopted her as his daughter."

"Was there no father then?" The brilliantly blue eyes
met hers searchingly and her own dropped away.

"He was drowned in a fishing boat off Cornwall," she
said in a soft hurry of words, but if he thought this had
disposed of Tabbie's father neatly he did not say so. He
did not say anything for a time and then he remarked that
it appeared that Sir Joseph Sackroyd was even a greater
villain than he had thought. Then rather quickly he
changed the subject to the conduct of the war and soon
after he took his leave.

"We shall meet in Scutari perhaps," he told Blanche as
he took her hand in farewell. "So I will not say goodbye."

After he had gone Blanche remarked to her brother,
"Did you ever see such an odd man? Though not without
charm. What did he mean, do you think, when he said Sir
Joseph killed his wife?"

Hubert smiled. "Lord Colleston likes to talk in riddles," he said. "And I am afraid I shall not try to guess the answer to them. I was pleased to attend to his physical condition when the need arose, but his private life is not my business."

The war news continued to throw long shadows over the nation and Sir Joseph began to read the newspaper to himself at breakfast instead of waiting to impart it to his wife and their nieces later. On the fourteenth of November, however, one glance at his face was sufficient to tell them that some catastrophe had occurred.

"What does it say, my love?" asked Lady Sackroyd at last in a trembling voice. "Tell me quickly. Is it bad news?"

"The worst we have had in weeks." He pushed aside his plate untouched. "Finish your breakfast—and you too, girls—and then we will repair to the morning-room as usual and I will read you what it says."

Left to themselves their anxiety mounted, and only Fanny enjoyed her breakfast that morning before they joined her uncle in the morning-room.

The fire in the grate smouldered dolefully with scarcely a spark in its heart and the yellow mist of a foggy November day pressed against the windows of the room. Sir Joseph adjusted his spectacles, cleared his throat, and read the despatch from the Crimea and Mr. Russell's account of the charge of the Light Brigade at Balaclava that had resulted in the loss of four hundred and nine men out of six hundred and seven. "Mind you," he added heavily with a glance at his wife's horror-stricken face, "it does not say here that all are killed. Some may have been made prisoner, and about eighty wounded have come in."

"Supposing Harry is among the dead?" Lady Sackroyd

burst into tears. "I must go to Louisa at once. Fanny my love, find Parker and tell her to pack her things. And, Tabbie, don't sit there staring at your uncle. Ring the bell and order the carriage to be ready to take me to Paddington Station as soon as possible."

While Fanny fled Tabbie did her best to soothe her aunt. "Louisa is with Harry's parents, dearest Aunt," she said, taking her hand in both of hers. "Would it not be better to leave her alone with them until we know more?"

"Nonsense! What an unfeeling creature you are, Tabbie!" Lady Sackroyd flung her hands away from her and dried her eyes. "I shall go to Louisa today: it is my duty as her mother."

"All the same I think Tabbie is right, my dear." Sir Joseph put down *Bradshaw's Railway Companion* in which he had been looking up the trains to Hampshire. "I think we should wait until Louisa sends for us. Your sudden arrival might alarm her."

"And Harry may have escaped," added Tabbie cheerfully.

But Harry had not escaped. His name came through in the list of officers who had been severely wounded, and some doubt was felt lest the hampers of good food and the champagne were any longer able to protect him. It was soon learned however that the badly wounded officers and men were to be sent home, and they had to wait for news that seemed as if it would never come.

With her aunt's frayed nerves to combat at home Tabbie was thankful for the duties of St. Ursula's that took her attention all day, and one morning at the beginning of December she had a curious experience there.

Mrs. Morrish knocked at the door of her little office

soon after she arrived and asked if she would see a gentleman who had called, asking for her.

"He would not give his name," said the head nurse. "But he asked for Miss Sackroyd."

Tabbie's thoughts went to William, who had promised to be with them for Christmas: she had heard from him frequently of late and in every letter he had asked for news of Blanche. Thinking he had come in person this time instead of writing she rose to welcome him and then stopped short seeing that her visitor was a stranger, and dressed moreover in the scarlet shell-jacket of a common soldier.

Her hand dropped to her side and she stood there in the cold December sunshine of the small window, her dark eyes studying him with grave enquiry, a half-smile on her lips. He was a tall man and under his forage cap his fair hair was turning white, while his eyes were a deep and startling blue in his lean face.

"You are Miss Sackroyd?" he asked. He was no common soldier she thought for all his uniform. His voice was pleasant and cultured and he had an air of authority.

"Yes, sir."

"Miss Tabitha Sackroyd?" he insisted. "Niece to Sir Joseph Sackroyd?"

"I am." He was looking at her so gravely that she became more puzzled still. It was as if he were trying to impress her features on his mind.

"Has your uncle any other nieces or nephews?"

"Oh yes, he has about a score." She laughed. "My aunt's family was a large one and all her sisters and brothers are married and have families."

"I did not mean your aunt's side of the family. Has

your uncle any nephews and nieces on his side—a brother's children for example—or possibly a sister's?"

"He had no brothers and only one sister—Tabitha— who was my mother." He saw a shadow pass over her face and her eyes clouded. "She died when I was a baby and my uncle adopted me. That is why I have his name."

"Was she living in London when she died? Forgive me if these questions sound impertinent, but I have my reasons for wishing to know."

"She died in Cornwall and she is buried there in a country churchyard—I believe the village is called Trevennick. But I have never been there and one of my cousins who visited it once told me that he could not find her grave. I think it may have been overgrown with grass, because you see there was nobody to care for it."

"Nobody to care?" The tone in which he spoke was charged with feeling.

"She died in the summer of 1830," she explained gently.

"Yes. Of course. It is a long time ago." He hesitated, studying her intently, and then he said abruptly: "May I ask two things of you, my dear? The first is that you do not mention my visit or the questions I have asked to any of your relatives?"

"I will promise you that with pleasure. My mother's history is not one that I care to discuss with anyone."

"Then you have been very forbearing with me." She waited for his second request and when it came it surprised her even more than the other. "Will you wish me Godspeed before I go? I sail for the Crimea in two days' time."

"But of course I will." She gave him her hand. "You are very mysterious, sir, but I think you may have known my mother once and that is why you have asked me these things. If you knew her—and were fond of her, as seems likely—then I will not hesitate to wish you Godspeed and a safe return."

He held her hand in his for a long moment and then with a stifled sigh he let it go. "God bless you," he said gently and the next moment he was gone.

She did not remember until later that she had not asked his name and when Jenny came for her that afternoon she stopped for a moment to ask the porter if her visitor had given it to him.

"Not to me, he didn't, Miss." The porter shook his head. "But 'is servant was here talking and telling me as 'is master and 'imself 'ad joined up as private sojers for to go and fight the Rooshans, and from what 'e let fall I 'ave the notion as the gentleman was a lord."

"A lord? And a private soldier?" It was a conundrum she could not solve and neither could he.

"Seemed queer like to me too, Miss, but maybe 'e was a bit soft-like if you take me meaning, and 'is man joined with 'im to keep an eye on 'im. Seemed to think a deal of 'im, 'e did."

Tabbie was glad to hear it. She did not know why her visitor had given her the impression that he was alone in the world, because if he was a lord it did not seem likely that he would be. And then the problems of the hospital came back to her and she dismissed him from her mind.

CHAPTER
13

That Christmas was a bleak one: festivities were limited and no court or ball-dresses were worn. Nobody had the heart to dance or dine under the shadow of the war, while in the streets chestnut sellers did the best trade as people stopped by their brightly burning braziers where hot shovels were giving off appetising smells, and where, as they stood eating hot chestnuts from cone-shaped bags, they could discuss the scanty war news in low voices.

Before William returned to Norfolk he spent an evening alone with Dr. Ashley. The two men smoked their cheroots contentedly and talked about Blanche.

The doctor had received one letter from his sister written soon after she had arrived in Scutari but he did not reveal what she had said in it even to William, because she had told him that Mr. Russell's recent reports had not been exaggerated. She had described their arrival at the old Turkish barracks that had been turned into the hospital, the enormous buildings, the courtyards full of refuse and filth, the cellars where prostitutes and children were lodged, the lack of beds and ordinary equipment, and their own quarters where each nurse was only allowed one small bowl of water a day to drink and to wash in, and where there were not even sacks between them and the stone floor and its cockroaches.

"At least we start with the advantages of health and strength," she wrote. *"But you were right, my dear brother, in guessing where our greatest adversaries would be."*

How ever many wounded and sick were brought in and left to die with wounds fast turning gangrenous, Miss Nightingale and her nurses were only permitted to watch and do nothing, so jealous were the army authorities of their power.

"Say nothing of this to anyone," Blanche added. *"Miss Nightingale will not allow us to open our lips in case we should be labelled as trouble makers and sent home without being able to lift a finger to help our poor men. She says—rather grimly I fear—that our time will come."*

The time came sooner than they thought. When William got home he wrote a long letter to Blanche, but by the time she received it that dedicated woman had little time to answer it, because the bitter winter had set in above Sevastopol and in the ensuing disaster to the British troops Miss Nightingale's nurses used every moment desperately sewing up great bags and stuffing them with straw to make some sort of beds for the sick that were pouring into the old Turkish barracks. The wards were full, the corridors lined with men lying on bare boards because even the straw had run out. They had no pillows and lay with their heads on their boots, on unwashed rotten floors crawling with vermin.

Sometimes at night when she could snatch a few hours' rest Blanche's thoughts would go to William and the letter that had brought tears to her eyes with its picture of his country house and English garden and of kind gentle William himself. She thought of the horror with which he would view the drainage system at Scutari. More than a thousand men were suffering from diarrhœa in the hospital and the water pipes that had flushed the privies, stopped up when the barracks were used for troops, had never been unstopped since. In the liquid filth floating over the floors, huge wooden tubs were provided in wards and corridors for the men to use and left unemptied by the orderlies for twenty-four hours on end. The hospital could be smelt outside the walls.

All this Blanche told her brother gradually later, as the appalling memories of Scutari came back to her when she was once again in the clean orderliness of her own home.

If it had not been for the large sum of money at Miss Nightingale's disposal, she told him, with which she bought provisions from Constantinople, one of the great markets of the world, far more men would have died. It was that money and those provisions that made the doctors surrender to her and her nurses.

During that terrible winter it was to Miss Nightingale that they went for the comfort and sustenance of their patients as it became known that if anything were needed it could usually be obtained from her personal stores, and it was issued by her upon requisition in the official form by a medical officer. By the end of December Miss Nightingale was in fact purveying the hospital.

And having thus gained recognition at last she did not stop there. Every day the wooden tubs would be emptied, the intrepid figure of Miss Nightingale standing beside them until it was done, and the floors were scrubbed and the men's clothes washed. Her efficiency was unquestioned, her spirit unquenchable, her authority absolute. She helped with amputations, dressed wounds—sometimes for eight hours at a stretch—and walked the wards continually, putting the men's needs above all petty jealousies and small minded criticism, and the men adored her, while powerless Authority bided its time.

In March the red-coated postman brought a second letter from Blanche to Dr. Ashley, saying that she had been ill with the Crimea fever and that Miss Nightingale was sending her home. She had begged to be allowed to stay but there were far too many sick and wounded men for sick nurses to be allowed to remain.

By the time the letter was received Blanche was at Marseilles and a week later she was in London. But she did not come alone: with her there travelled a soldier from the heights of Sevastopol with a shell splinter lodged in his spine.

"Hubert!" Blanche scarcely waited to greet her brother before taking him out to the carriage, "I have brought Lord Colleston with me. I knew you would not object if he beraks his journey with us for a few nights before going on to Westmorland. He wanted to travel on to Euston Station tonight but I did not think it possible. His servant is with him: miraculously he escaped everything except Crimea fever, and he was allowed to travel with his master as an extra hospital orderly."

"Where is Lord Colleston? In the carriage?" Hubert hurried out and with his man assisted Bates to carry the sick man into the house and upstairs to one of the spare bedrooms, where Mrs. Webb was setting the housemaids on to getting the bed ready and a fire lighted, though the evening was a mild one.

Richard Colleston did not protest: he was, as Blanche had said, a very sick man, and his back was causing him agony, although only the greyness of his face and a slight twitch of a muscle in his jaw as they moved him gave any identification of this. Hubert stayed to help Bates to get him into bed and said that he would examine him in the morning. "In the meantime my prescription is a light meal, a glass of brandy, and a good sleep," he said.

He left the thin and emaciated Bates to make him comfortable, and then he went down to the drawing-room to see his sister who was sitting there in her travelling clothes as if she had not the strength to untie her bonnet strings or loosen her shawl.

"My dear Blanche!" He gently took the bonnet from her head and then exclaimed at her cropped appearance. "My dear, what have they done to your hair?"

"We kept our hair short because of the lice," she told him. "But when I went down with the fever Miss Nightingale thought it best to cut it off. It is growing again now though, and I am feeling a great deal stronger." She smiled at him bravely. "I was glad to have Lord Colleston with me on the journey: we looked after each other and Bates looked after us both. Lord Colleston is going to buy his release from the Army so that he will not have to go back."

The following morning she came down to breakfast much refreshed however, and her brother was able to report that he had looked in at their guest and had been told that he had passed a good night.

"Hubert," said Blanche anxiously, "I am afraid he is

very desperately ill. He cannot walk—and in fact he cannot feel anything from the waist downwards."

"So I understand." The doctor was more reassuring than he felt. "I have told him that he is to stay here for at least a week before attempting the journey to Westmorland, and I have written a note to Sir Thomas Shriber asking him to come and see him this afternoon. Sir Thomas has made a study of spinal complaints."

Blanche was sufficiently cheered by this to visit St. Ursula's during the morning, and she was encouraged to learn that not only had the linen room not suffered by her absence, but that the store cupboards were as complete as she had kept them and that all the records of the patients' progress had been faithfully written down in Tabbie's neat handwriting.

Tabbie was delighted to see her, although she too mourned the loss of Blanche's hair, and she was also worried because her friend looked so ill. Blanche made light of it, however, and before she went on to see Mrs. Morrish she asked after the Sackroyds. "I understand from Hubert that Harry Rawlings is home?"

"Yes, he came home in February. He has lost a leg."

"So I heard, but the officers' hospital in Balaclava had nothing to complain of and I knew he would be well nursed there. How has Louisa taken it?"

"As well as I knew she would, in spite of my aunt's lamentations, and her accusations of heartlessness when I suggested that Louisa would rather have a husband without a leg than no husband at all!" Tabbie laughed but there was a rather wry sound in it and Blanche looked at her sharply. She wondered what had been going on in her absence, knowing nothing of Fanny and how she had taken Tabbie's place with every encouragement from her aunt.

New dresses had been purchased generously for the rabbit-toothed Fanny. "Tabbie is at her old hospital all day so I am very sure she has no need for new dresses," thus Lady Sackroyd reproached Tabbie through Fanny. Fanny must go with them to the play and the opera. "Tabbie will be much too tired to accompany us after her day at St. Ursula's." And Fanny was to be the daughter of the house now that "Tabbie has lost all interest in her home."

Tabbie said nothing of this to Blanche: she was only glad to have her back again and looked forward to handing over the office to her when she felt strong enough, so that she could return to the linen room.

CHAPTER
14

Blanche said nothing to Tabbie about the patient she had brought home with her, but he remained in her thoughts all day so that she found it difficult to concentrate on what Mrs. Morrish told her, and on those of the patients who remembered her. In those few months more than half their number had been sent home to indifferent lodgings because they were no longer ill enough to be kept at the hospital, and two had died, and there were new ones to be greeted and talked to and put at ease.

She left as soon as she could, asking Tabbie to take charge, too impatient to wait for the carriage. She found Sir Thomas's carriage before the door of their house and she had to wait upstairs in her drawing-room for what seemed ages before he left. He appeared then to have an almost endless conversation with Hubert in the hall before the front door was finally opened for him and he drove away.

She waited with impatience for her brother to come upstairs to her. "Hubert!" she cried as he came into the room. "That was Sir Thomas—I recognised his carriage. What does he say about Lord Colleston? Does he hold out any hope of his recovery?"

"Hush! Not so loud, my dear." Hubert told her to sit down. "First of all Lord Colleston is to remain here for a time before continuing his journey. Sir Thomas does not advise moving him until the end of next week."

"But—will he recover?" asked Blanche.

Hubert hesitated before replying and then he said quietly, "I am afraid as you suspected, my dear, Lord Colleston is gravely ill. The splinter, lodged in the spine, cannot be removed by any kind of operation: it would result in instant death. But unfortunately the area round the wound has become diseased, and it is only a question of time—perhaps a month or even less—before it must kill him."

Blanche closed her eyes for a moment and went so white that he thought she would faint. "I did not mean to tell you until after he had gone back to Westmorland," he said. "There is no reason why I should have distressed you . . ."

"I am glad you told me," she said. "Because now I know that there is something I must do. You see, on the voyage home he told me why he hated Sir Joseph Sackroyd, and if—he is to die so soon—I think there is a deep wrong that must be put right." And sitting there in the warm sunshine of the early spring day, she told him what it was.

"You are going to lose me one of my best patients," he told her when she had finished. "But you are right to do it. In fact I do not see how you can do anything else. Will you go to see Sir Joseph or will you invite him here?"

"I shall ask him to come here," she said. "And I shall fetch Tabbie from St. Ursula's before he comes."

"You will prepare Lord Colleston I hope?"

"We talked it over on the journey and although he was as certain as anyone could be of what had happened in the past he wished to see his lawyer before anything was put in train. But—will there be time?"

"He sent Bates to Lincoln's Inn this morning with a message to Mr. Tracy to come tomorrow."

"Then we must wait till he has seen him before I write to Sir Joseph."

"And Tabbie? If it is as you say, will you prepare her?"

"No. She must come to it with an open mind, because it is she who must ultimately make a choice, and he did not wish her to be prejudiced for or against either of them. He was insistent that she must be free to choose."

"His lordship is more magnanimous than I would be in his shoes."

Tabbie was surprised when her uncle asked her at breakfast one morning if she knew why Miss Ashley wished to see him.

"No," she said. "She has said nothing to me about it." She was more surprised still when soon after she arrived at St. Ursula's that same morning the doctor's carriage arrived to take her to his house, where Blanche was waiting for her. Apart from telling her rather brusquely that his sister wanted her Hubert was uncommunicative, and as Blanche came out to greet her he drove on.

"I sent for you, my dear," Blanche said as she took Tabbie indoors, "because there is somebody staying here that I would like you to meet—or rather, somebody who wishes to meet you."

She took her bonnet and shawl from her and led the way upstairs to the quiet of the second floor and the spare bedroom where a man was lying propped up on pillows in the big four-poster. He turned his head eagerly at their entrance.

"This is Lord Colleston, Tabbie," Blanche said. She pushed a chair forward for her beside the bed. "He has something to tell you." And to Lord Colleston, "This is Miss Tabitha Sackroyd, Lord Colleston. I will leave her with you."

"Thank you, Miss Ashley."

She gave Tabbie's shoulder a little encouraging pat and then the door closed behind her, and the girl sat down in the chair, suddenly recognising the occupant of the bed.

"Why," she said smiling, "I have met you before!"

"I called on you at the little hospital down the road where you were busy with accounts, and very businesslike you looked too." His eyes rested on her tenderly. "It was the week before I left for the Crimea."

"You asked me some questions about my mother."

"And you were kind enough to tell me what I wanted to know, although you admitted later that it was painful to you." He frowned and was silent for a moment as if wondering how to start, and then he said abruptly: "I had heard from Miss Ashley and her brother that Sir Joseph Sackroyd had an adopted niece and the incredible thought came to me that this niece might be Tabitha Sackroyd's daughter, and that in such a case, she was mine as well."

"Yours?" Tabbie's startled eyes took in the wasted face, the fair hair going white, the deep blue gaze that met her own. "You mean—you thought you might be my father?"

"I fancied so. That's why I asked you those questions that day, because I wanted to instruct my man of business to go to Cornwall in my absence abroad, and to search the parish registers in some of the parishes there to try to discover if a lady by the name of Tabitha Satterthwaite had died there twenty-four years ago."

Tabitha Satterthwaite. Tabbie thought of her mother's locket with the curl of fair hair and the initials R.A.S.

"Please go on," she said gently.

"Tracy—that is my lawyer—came to see me here yesterday and he confirmed that my wife had died at Trevennick in the summer of 1830. There was no record of any child having been baptised there however, and when Sir Joseph wrote to me that summer informing me in a few curt lines that Tabitha was dead, he did not mention the child either. But Tracy discovered that there were those in the village who remembered the baby's birth—notably the midwife, and a doctor from Truro, who had been sent for because it was a difficult case. He told Tracy that the mother had been so exhausted that when she asked him to baptise the child he had not hesitated to do so, thinking that neither of them might last until morning. He baptised the child by the name of Tabitha, and the mother told him that she was not a Mrs. Smith, but a Mrs. Satterthwaite, and that the child was the daughter of her husband, Richard Algernon Satterthwaite. She made him promise to keep it from the world and he had done so, until my man Tracy saw him and explained what had happened."

"But why did my uncle not tell you about me?" Tabbie tried to assimilate the things that were being revealed to her and found it difficult. The man on the bed gave a wry smile.

"I suppose he did not think I could be trusted to bring up his sister's child, and angry as I am with him for having deprived me of you all these years, I can see what was in his mind." He was determined to be impartial, and to present everything to her as it had occurred. "When I married your mother I was a depraved young rascal—a younger son with no thought of inheriting titles or estates. I had run through a fortune of my own, and my father refused to pay any more of my debts. He said he was not going to pay any longer for a drunkard and a gambler, and when he died I found that he had kept his word, leaving me only enough to subsist on. So that you can see for yourself that with such a reputation as mine and such an inheritance, your uncle could scarcely welcome me as his only sister's husband. He was her guardian after all and a rich man: a Yorkshire man moreover, and fond of his 'brass.' He did not intend to be his sister's banker in order to supply a profligate and penniless husband with money, and for that nobody can blame him." He paused, looking at her anxiously, as if she must agree with him that it had not been her uncle's fault, and then as she did not reply he continued:

"It did not occur to him that I was genuinely in love with his sister, as she was with me. I would have cheerfully given my life for her, and when we ran off together to get married I swore that I would reform, with her help, and I meant it. But her brother was not to know that, and I daresay if he had he would have felt the promises of a waster like myself were not worth much. So he followed us and he found us in a village in Scotland, and he accused me of every evil thing he could think of—and of some that others had thought of for him—in front of his sister. He begged her to leave me and dared me to deny his accusations. I did not deny them. I reminded her that I had already told her what my life had been and what sort of fellow I was, but she could only listen to her brother. He had always dominated her and she had been accustomed from childhood to look up to him and to obey him. I believe she was very frightened of him. At all events in the finish I lost my temper and told her that she must choose between us. Either she went with her brother that day or she stayed with me. But if she left me I said I would never recognise her or acknowledge her to be my wife. She scarcely hesitated. She packed her things and she left with her brother, travelling post, and I never heard from her or saw her again."

There was silence in the room for a long moment. Then Tabbie said gently, "Did you not write to her?"

"I did after she left and I had time to think it over and to realise how young she was and how much in her brother's hands. I implored her to think of what she was doing, I told her that I loved her more than I had ever loved any woman before, and that I would love her till I died. It sounds romantic rubbish from this distance perhaps, but I meant what I said. I had my letter returned to me, with a note from her brother saying that she did not wish me to write again. I have wondered since if she ever received that letter. It was about a fortnight afterwards when my own family matters suddenly took a turn that needed all my energy and all my attention. My elder brother and his two young sons who had been mountaineering in the French Alps were killed in an avalanche. My sister-in-law and her daughters were left distracted in a small inn in Chamonix and I had to hurry to them.

There were the bodies to be brought home and interred in the family vault, there were my sister-in-law and my nieces to look after and to provide for, and I had scarcely time to stop to consider that the title and estates were now mine. The knowledge gave me no pleasure but it made me determined to show the world that I could and would reform: I buried myself in Westmorland and set myself the task of learning to know my neighbours—none of whom took kindly to me at first. I gave up all my former acquaintances and seldom came to London, keeping the house in Cavendish Square empty except for a housekeeper and a few servants. It was on one of my rare visits to London that I was set upon one night and rescued from the gutter where the ruffians had left me by Dr. Ashley and his sister. From them later on I learned of your existence."

Her grave and thoughtful eyes told him nothing and he moved impatiently and hurt his back and winced. He had done his best to be impartial and to remember, as Blanche had warned him, that the Sackroyds' house had been Tabbie's home all her life. He was too proud to appeal to her emotions or to tell her how much her uncle hated him. He said quietly:

"Miss Ashley asked me to tell you the whole truth of my part in this unhappy business. I believe she has sent for your uncle to let him tell you his side of the story. It is not one that reflects well on my behaviour, Tabbie—if I may call you that. But it happens to be true. And as you are my daughter I would like to acknowledge you as such before—I should say, even if I—damn it, my dear, it is only natural I suppose. But you may not agree. You may say, after hearing your uncle, that it is better to have no father than one with such a reputation as mine."

She put her hand on the coverlet in a moment of protest. "Don't!" she said. "I will hear my uncle—and then I will come and see you again."

"Very well." He closed his eyes and without the brilliance of that blue fire upon her she managed to get herself out of the room. She found Bates waiting outside.

"Miss Ashley said I was to tell you, m'lady, that Sir Joseph is here," he said.

The form of address startled her, and a prey to many misgivings she walked downstairs to the drawing-room.

Her uncle was standing by the fireplace with Blanche in a chair on the opposite side. Her face was extremely grave while his was mystified and annoyed.

"Ah there you are, Tabbie," he said as she came into the room. "Miss Ashley tells me I have something to say to you, but I'm hanged if I know what it can be."

"I expect it is about my father," Tabbie said quietly.

His head came up with a shock of surprise and seeing the expression on her face he was unusually unsure of himself.

"Why, my dear," he said, blustering, "I am sure there is nothing more to be said about him. He died, as you know."

"I know the story that was put about," Tabbie said. "It was a story that nobody believed, although I was credulous enough to think that it was true until quite recently. It never occurred to me that you had lied to me for twenty-four years."

"It was for your own good," he protested.

"No doubt you thought it was," she conceded. "But now that I have seen my father and heard his side of the story I would like to hear yours, if you please."

His jaw dropped. "He—is here?" he said incredulously.

"I have just come from him. I know that my mother ran away with him and married him, and that you followed them and persuaded her to leave him. That is all he would tell me. I am waiting to hear your side of it now."

Sir Joseph scowled. From the cool way the chit was looking at him she might be his judge and he a criminal in the dock.

"Would you like me to go, Tabbie?" asked Blanche.

"No thank you. Please stay."

Her uncle took a turn about the room and ended up at the window twisting the blind cord in his hands.

"When my father died," he told her, "your mother was left in my charge. I was ten years older than she was and there were no other children. Our mother was delicate and died when Tabitha was born. I was devoted to my sister and my wife said I spoilt her and perhaps I did. She was such a pretty little girl. But when she was sixteen and I had not long been married she developed a most unruly spirit, being impertinent to my wife and refusing to marry a young man who was the son of my father's oldest friend, with enough brass to pave our High Street here. Nothing I could threaten her with—even to turning her out of doors—would make her change her mind, and at last my wife suggested she should go to boarding school to be taught discipline. I agreed for the sake of peace and harmony in my home, but I regretted it later because it was at this school that she became friends with a Miss Maud Satterthwaite, a distant relative of Lord Colleston. She went to stay with Miss Satterthwaite that Christmas and fell in love with a dissolute young cousin of hers—a younger brother of Colleston's heir—a man who had been disowned by his father for his evil ways. They corresponded without my knowledge and in the following spring she eloped with him to Scotland. I was furious and I went after them vowing I would kill the man but when I caught them my anger had become a cold determination to get her away from him at all costs. I ordered her to leave him, telling her that he was only after her money, that he was a dissipated rascal and the black sheep of his family, that he drank and gambled, that he had one mistress in Paris and another in London, and that once she got over her infatuation for him she would never know another happy moment. And I warned her that if she defied me I would not rest until I had got him behind bars in a debtors' prison. He swore he did not know that she had any money—a damned lie—but he admitted the truth of most of the rest, swearing he would reform if she would stay with him, but he saw that she was terrified of me and that he would never prevail against me with his wife. Wife indeed! She was under age and she could not marry without my consent and he knew it."

"Is the law not different in Scotland, sir?" asked Blanche mildly. "Surely there was no doubt in their minds that they had been legally married?"

"I daresay. I do not know." He dismissed her interruption resentfully. "My threat of the Marshalsea worked, however, and I took her home with me, but of course soon afterwards my wife discovered she was expecting a child and refused to have her to live with us where all our friends would gossip about her. So I took a cottage for her in Cornwall and engaged a woman who had once been her nurse to look after her. You, Tabbie, were born in the following April, and three months later your mother died of some wasting illness, I never knew what it was. I saw that she was buried decently down there in Trevennick and I brought you back with me and I wrote and told your father that Tabitha was dead. I did not hear from him—indeed I did not expect to hear. He was a heartless monster, young as he was. I gave you my name as my adopted daughter, although your aunt did not like it, and to quieten gossip invented the story of the naval officer who was supposed to have been drowned. I did not repudiate it, for your sake as well as ours. I have looked upon you more as a daughter than a niece, Tabbie, and although lately I have felt you have not rewarded your aunt's affection as well as you might, my home is still yours. If anyone dares to censure my conduct I can only say I would do the same again in the same circumstances."

He stopped speaking, looking at his niece, whose back was to the room, her forehead bent on her arms that were resting on the high chimney piece.

"Well, Tabbie?" he said impatiently to that slender, motionless back. "Do you blame me? If you have seen your father this morning I daresay he lied to you as easily as he lied to your mother years ago. A leopard does not change his spots. But I can assure you that whatever he said to you I have told you nothing that is not true."

"He told me much the same story." Tabbie spoke without lifting her head and Blanche regarded her with compassion. The girl needed time in which to assess the whole sorry business, and there was no time. She said aloud, "It seems, Sir Joseph, that history repeats itself. Tabbie must make the choice between you and her father as her mother had to do before her."

"Then Tabbie shall choose," said Sir Joseph, his voice confident and assured. There appeared to be little doubt in his mind of the outcome.

It was at this moment that Bates opened the door. "I

beg your pardon, Miss," he said to Blanche. "The doctor has returned and would like to see her ladyship before she goes upstairs."

"Very well, Bates," said Blanche, but it was Tabbie, lifting her head quickly, who said, "I will come and see the doctor now, Bates." She did not look at her uncle as she left the room.

" 'Her ladyship'?" Sir Joseph repeated the words stupidly. "Miss Ashley, that fellow . . ."

"Gave Tabbie her rightful title," said Blanche quietly. "Were you surprised? Surely you knew that she was Lady Tabitha Satterthwaite, as she was soon after she was born?"

"I didn't give it a thought." He was shocked, even horrified. "There was a brother and there were two nephews between Richard Satterthwaite and the title." He stared unhappily at the pleasant suburban road beyond the gates, with its paved centre and hedges on either side. "I know there were because I made enquiries."

Blanche did not question it. "You said that Richard Satterthwaite was after your sister's money," she said. "Had she a large fortune?"

"Twenty thousand pounds. But if she died before she was twenty-one it was to come to me." He added hastily, exonerating himself, "I gave Tabbie board and lodging and I settled five hundred pounds of the money on her. What more could I do? I suppose you think I should have made enquiries about her father from time to time but knowing what I did about the man I was not going to hand my niece over to a reprobate. Do you find that unforgiveable?"

Without answering the question she said: "One thing you have made plain to me, Sir Joseph, is that your

hatred for Richard Satterthwaite was far stronger than
your love for your sister. I am not your judge, but I do
find it inexcusable that a girl of good family should have
been brought up in your house with the stigma of illegiti-
macy hanging over her. How ever much you disliked her
father the pettiness of such a revenge was contemptible."

"Illegitimate? Tabbie?" His astonishment appeared to
be genuine. "I've never heard about that."

"But I'm sure your friends knew about it—and your
wife."

He did not anwer. He took up his hat, turned it in his
clumsy hands a turn or two, staring at her all the time in
a dazed fashion, and then he went heavily away.

In the meantime Tabbie went downstairs to where
Hubert was waiting for her. He got up quickly as she entered the room and put a chair for her near his writing-
table.

"Lady Tabitha," he said, "please sit down."

"No," she said distressed. "Not that—not from you! I
am still the same Tabbie that I was yesterday."

"But things have changed," he reminded her gently. "If
you prefer it I will compromise and call you Lady Tabbie.
Is that more friendly?"

"Much more friendly, although to me you will still be
Blanche's brother—Hubert." She drew a deep breath. "I
suppose you wish to speak to me about my father?"

"Yes, my dear, I'm afraid I must. There has been no
time to tell you the details, but Lord Colleston was badly
wounded out there in the Crimea and I sent for Sir
Thomas Shriber to examine him the day after Blanche
brought him here. Unhappily he confirmed my own opinion—that the splinter of shell lodged in the spine is
causing infection in the area around it which is gradually

spreading." He broke off. "In short, there is nothing we can do to stop it or to cure it."

"How long will it be?" She spoke bravely, her eyes dry and he knew she could bear the truth.

"Perhaps a month—perhaps a little longer. One cannot tell."

She gave a small quivering sigh. "And I have only known him today. There have been twenty-four years lost to us. I shall never forgive my aunt and uncle for this."

He could not comfort her there, just as he could not think of what the Sackroyds had done to her calmly or reasonably. There were more warnings that he must give her, however, before he let her go.

"Your father intends to travel north next week. I presume you will go with him?"

"Can you ask that? When I have missed him all my life, I could not leave him now."

"I am glad of it for his sake, but for yours I am sorry it has to happen like this, because you will witness a great deal of suffering—a great deal of pain. I will give you opiates for him before I leave you with him, but they must be sparingly used. It may help you to know that I have promised to travel with you to Westmorland: my sister and I thought it would not only help Bates, but you too, Lady Tabbie."

She smiled at him sadly. "You knew in advance what my decision would be?"

"Yes." Knowing her as he did he had known too that she could make no other. "And now if you are ready, shall I take you to your father?"

"Thank you." She was quite composed, though for a moment outside her father's door that composure cracked a little, and she caught his hand whispering something that sounded like, "Pray for me, dear Hubert, that I may have courage!" before she went in and the door closed behind her.

Her father was watching for her and as she came into the room and sat down beside him he said impatiently: "Well, child? Did you hear him? Which is it to be, your uncle or me?"

"There was never any choice." She smiled at him serenely. "Surely you knew that? My place is here, with you, Papa." She leant forward rather shyly to kiss him.

He gripped her shoulder and kept her there, looking into her eyes. "You're not doing this from a sense of duty?" He tried desperately to be fair to the man he hated. "Your uncle's house has been your home all your life. You must have affection for it?"

Affection for a glass palace? She might as well have affection for Paddington Station. "My uncle's house was never a home to me," she said quietly.

"But your aunt? You love her no doubt . . ."

"She has never loved me." She took his hand in hers. "No, you will not get rid of me so easily I'm afraid, Papa, now that I have found you and know that you are my own."

"Tabbie!" He drew her down until her head rested on his shoulder. "It is like some miracle. I'm damned glad those ruffians attacked me that night and left me for dead in the gutter, otherwise I'd have never been rescued by Ashley and learned through his sister that I had a daughter." He studied her face tenderly. "You are like your mother—and yet you are like me too. You have got my mother's hair. But I daresay that fellow—your uncle you know—meant well."

"They say hell is paved with good intentions, and

though I will not call my uncle's house a hell, Papa, the pavement was sometimes a little hard." Addy's dresses, the dinners in the school-room, the glances of their friends, the whole brittle life in the glass palace that her aunt had made.

He laughed delightedly. "Now I know that you are my daughter. What a pleasure it will be to take you home with me, to introduce you to our friends in Westmorland and to the family. They will like you, Tabbie, and you will like them. You can ride of course?"

"No. My uncle did not have me taught horse-riding."

"Never mind. I will teach you myself once I'm free of this damned splinter. It will work its way out, I tell these medical fellows. It will work its way out."

Sir Joseph arrived home to find his wife impatiently waiting to hear what Blanche Ashley wanted with him, and she listened with mounting anger when he told her what had happened and that Lord Colleston had claimed Tabbie for his daughter.

"I must say it startled me to hear the servant speak of her as a 'ladyship'," he added resentfully. "I did not know that Richard Satterthwaite had succeeded to the title. I thought there was a brother and two nephews before him."

"They were killed in an accident in the French Alps." She did not meet his eyes. "I read about it at the time in the social news of the *Courier*—I showed it to you I am sure."

"And I am sure that you did not." He spoke warmly. "When did this happen?"

"Oh, years ago. When Tabbie was a baby."

"All that time?" He was shocked.

"Well what of it?" Her voice rose. "It was not likely that a man with that character would have troubled himself about the upbringing of a daughter. He would only have been too glad to have handed her over to us to keep, and as a result she would have taken precedence over our daughters. It would have been 'Lady Tabitha this' and 'Lady Tabitha that'—not just plain little Tabbie Sackroyd, nobody's daughter—and she would have had much finer clothes than our girls, and valuable jewellery and she would have been presented at a Drawing-Room by her grand relatives, and we would have had to give balls for her. Oh, there would have been no end to it and our poor girls would have been nowhere."

For a moment he was speechless, and then his anger broke and he rounded on her furiously. "You damned fool, do you not see how much it would have been to their advantage—to *our* advantage—to have been so closely related to an earl's daughter? And instead you have not only incurred the family's emmity but when this gets out I shall be surprised if we have one friend left in Kensington. No wonder Miss Ashley spoke with such contempt."

"Miss Ashley? What has she to do with it?"

"She told me that our friends here have taken it for granted all these years that Tabbie was illegitimate, and that the story of the naval officer was untrue. Were you aware of this?"

"Well of course I knew there was a lot of talk—there was bound to be. But I did not think it mattered. And as for Blanche Ashley, I don't see what business it is of hers." Her ladyship rounded on her husband in her turn. When had he ever troubled to hide his own hatred for

Tabbie's father? Why had he suppressed the child's birth in the first place instead of informing Richard Satterthwaite? Had she not had all the trouble of bringing Tabbie up from a baby—although she had never liked her, horrid, red-haired little thing. But he had not cared about that as long as he thought her father was a penniless rascal: it was only now when he found out he was an earl that he thought of all the advantages he might have given them. Well, it was a pity he had not thought of that before. It was perhaps fortunate that at that moment they were interrupted by a servant bringing a note from Tabbie to her aunt. It was very short.

"My dear Aunt Agatha," she wrote, *"my uncle will have told you that my father, Lord Colleston, is here in Dr. Ashley's house, seriously ill. My duty is clearly at his side—as it has been, unknown to us both, for the past twenty-four years. I shall be obliged if you will tell Jenny to pack only necessary articles of my clothing and to bring them to me here with the locket that was my mother's. I want nothing else. I hope when I am calmer I shall be able to remember the not unhappy days I spent with my cousins and to believe that what you and my uncle did for me was inspired by affection for my mother and not by your hatred for my father.*

Sincerely, your niece, Tabitha Satterthwaite."

CHAPTER

15

It may have been the care of his daughter that prolonged Lord Colleston's life to three months instead of one. With Bates to help her she nursed him continually, sleeping in the dressing-room next to his large bedroom with the door open between them so that she could be summoned if she were needed at any time in the night. The little maid Jenny, having delivered her belongings at the Ashleys only returned to the Sackroyd mansion to give in her notice to the housekeeper and pack her own box before joining Tabbie. Even Bates admitted that her rosy face and cheerful manner did a great deal to keep up their spirits at that sad time.

When Lord Colleston died Hubert went up to Westmorland for the funeral and he was asked up to the Castle to meet the new Earl and the ladies, and when he returned to London Blanche was anxious to know if he had seen Tabbie. How was she looking, she asked, and had the strain told upon her very much?

"I did not see her," Hubert said, "except once in the grounds before I left. I thought I saw her walking there with the new Countess. There were a great meany Satterthwaites there, my dear, but I had the impression that the family had closed its ranks and that Tabbie was safely inside that circle, protected from the world. All that Lady Colleston said to me was something about their gratitude to us—to you and me—for having found the late Earl's daughter, and that she thought we must have been God sent. She was so gracious, so kind, so charming that old as she was I think I would have lost my heart to her if . . ." He broke off.

"If it had not been another's already?" Blanche said gently.

"Why yes, I suppose you might say that." His voice grated a little. "I know now where she gets that charm from, our little Tabbie. Her father's family has it, as her father had it. It is something you cannot lay your finger on: it is there and it captivates you—while it holds you almost at arm's length."

"I know." Blanche's eyes were on the fire, because although it was July the evening was chilly enough for a fire after a day of rain. "When I accompanied Lord Colleston home from the Crimea and he told me his story I knew exactly why Tabbie's mother had run away with him. The only thing that I could not understand," she added in a low voice, "was how she could have left him."

Hubert glanced at her sharply. Then he said casually, "She was very much afraid of her brother I think. Sir Joseph has always been a bigot and a bit of a bully, as we know, but as a younger man he must have been quite intolerable." They were silent for a time and then Blanche said: "William Sackroyd came to see me while you were away. He was very upset about what had happened and blamed his parents very much. I tried to say that they had acted for what they thought was best for Tabbie, but I don't think he believed me."

After a moment she went on: "William came to see me about something else. He wrote to me while I was at Scutari and I am afraid I did not answer his letter. There was no time—and afterwards"—Afterwards there had been Lord Colleston and Tabbie.

Her brother said quietly, "He told me he was going to write. He wanted to marry you, Blanche."

"Yes." That letter, with its breath of a peaceful country house and garden, coming into all the squalor and filth and horror of Scutari. "He still does, Hubert. I asked him to give him time. Dear William, he has a very humble opinion of himself. He said in his letter that he had been in love with me since that day when we visited him in Norfolk. Sophy's children tearing about his garden and filling his rooms with their voices made him feel that he wanted a wife and children of his own. And when I came with you that day he knew that I was the woman he wanted for his wife. He said he had been nervous of speaking to me before I left England because he knew how dedicated I was to helping others and to nursing the sick and so on. I am afraid I let him think today that I was still—dedicated."

Her brother watched her with compassion, but he said nothing and presently she went on:

"He said he wanted to come directly he heard I was home, but there was the trouble about Tabbie and her father and he decided to wait until it had blown over a little in the Sackroyd household. I'm afraid, Hubert, they have transferred their allegiance to Dr. Philpot."

"I shall not grieve over that. It is in my mind to move back to London. Would you mind that, Blanche? There are some nice houses in Wimpole Street: it is a pleasant thoroughfare and near Regent's Park for our walks together. You might even find a use for your services in the ladies' hospital in Harley Street."

She shook her head. "I would like real nursing—the work that the old dames do in our hospitals. Miss Nightingale is certain that if ladies performed that work, being trained in nursing first by other nurses with many years of experience, there would be a vast field for the talents and care of educated women who are now fitted for nothing except being nursery governesses to the children of the rich. But to superintend or to mend linen only—no. That awful hospital at Scutari cured me of that. The lives that could have been saved and were lost through sheer ignorance and bad nursing. It does not bear thinking about." Her eyes darkened and he knew that she was thinking of one particular patient who had been there.

The housekeeper here came to ask if he were able to see a patient who had sent for him from Chelsea. "I told the man that you were only just home," she said with an anxious glance at the doctor's face. "You look tired, sir. Shall I tell him that you will call in the morning?"

"No, I will go now. I shall not want the carriage. The walk will do me good."

As Mrs. Webb left the room he dropped his hand on his sister's shoulder and gave it a gentle pressure.

"He didn't suffer very much towards the end," he told her gently. "The opiates deadened the pain—and Tabbie was with him. He died content."

Poor William, he thought, as he turned his steps towards Cheyne Walk later. He would have liked him for a brother-in-law and he thought Blanche would have been happy with him. But given time she might come to think of him seriously. He hoped so at all events, because it was a pity that two such nice people who could be happy together should spend their lives apart.

The autumn came and the move to the house in Wimpole Street was made: it was a charming town house with a small garden in the rear, and the little shops of Marylebone High Street conveniently near. And because they were no longer living near his parents, William became a more frequent visitor, until Blanche got into the habit of putting his rough hair tidy and pulling his cravat back from where it had wandered as Tabbie had done. She did not forget the man who had made such a deep impression on her during that voyage home from the Crimea, but gradually the memory of the arresting blue eyes faded a little, and she began to wonder if William was not right after all, and if it might not be a happy solution to their problems if his home became hers.

His happiness outweighed his parents' declaration that they would never receive him or his wife into their house again, and one day in November Blanche walked round with her brother to Marylebone Church and was there given into William's keeping. The Hippenstalls were there, and Addy and her husband came and Augustus, to wish his brother luck, and after a small wedding breakfast at which a beaming Mrs. Webb presided William and his bride set out for Shoreditch Station en route for Norfolk.

As they started off in the railway carriage that had been reserved for them William did not mention drains once, except to assure Blanche that even the cess-pool was now in perfect order.

"That is a great relief," she said. He turned his head and met her smiling eyes with a grin.

"I believe you are laughing at me," he said.

She slipped her hand into his arm. "Dearest William," she said. "I will always laugh with you—but at you, never."

"What will Hubert do without you?" he asked, not really bothered about it because Hubert must fend for himelf.

"He has an excellent housekeeper," said Blanche, and she did not seem unduly worried over her brother either.

But that did not stop the Wimpole Street house from being rather empty after all the guests had gone. As the days went by Hubert missed Blanche's needlework on the tables, the flowers in the rooms, the rustle of her dress on the stairs, and her touch on the piano. They were all things for which the excellent Mrs. Webb could not compensate him.

When Christmas came, however, it was a different story: he was invited warmly to West Bassett, with the promise that the Hippenstalls would be there too. It was enough, he told his sister, to make him decide not to go, but the happiness of her letter was irresistible.

He packed a portmanteau with things for the children and Sophy and Sam and for his sister and William, and he left Mrs. Webb in charge and started out one snowy morning for Norfolk. The train became colder as it travelled towards Norwich and foot-warmers cooled quickly. If it had not been for his fur travelling rug and the excellent hamper and the bottle of wine that Mrs. Webb had provided he would have arrived frozen.

At first he thought nobody was there to meet him and

then he caught sight of William, and behind him a familiar figure waiting to take his luggage.

He greeted William first and then, scarcely believing his eyes, held out his hand to the man behind him. "Bates! This is an unexpected pleasure!"

"We are here for Christmas, sir," Bates told him. "Her ladyship and Jenny and me." As Bates hurried off to collect the portmanteau William smiled at Hubert's astonished face.

"Blanche wrote to Tabbie, asking her to come," he explained. "The poor girl would have had to spend Christmas among all her relations at the Castle and kind though they may be we thought she needed something a little more comfortable."

Hubert thought of the luxury of the Castle with a twitch of his mouth, but he agreed gravely, and he was conscious of a quicker beat to his pulse as he joined William in his carriage, leaving Bates to follow with the luggage in the dog-cart.

It was dark when they arrived and the lamps were lighted in hall and rooms. Tabbie was in the drawing-room helping the children to dress a tall Christmas tree. Her black velvet dress made her bright hair look like a coil of copper on her neck. She gave her hand gravely to Hubert and said that it was good to see him again.

"I have missed you so much," she said, and although the words were spoken much as her great-aunt would have said them, with charm and perhaps with sincerity, they pleased him beyond all reason.

During the evening he did not have a chance to talk to her much. Others demanded his attention and the children were noisy little ruffians, excited and eager to join in all the Christmas games. They gathered round the kitchen table for snap-dragon, pulling the raisins out of the burning brandy with shrieks of delight, and then the mummers came and acted their play in the hall, being given quantities of ale afterwards in the kitchen and ending up in the ditch on the way home.

It was not until the next day when they took the children off for a walk in the snowy woods that Hubert had the opportunity for talking to Tabbie at all. He learned from her that the Satterthwaites regarded themselves as her own family and that the Sackroyds had not even sent a word of good wishes. He also learned that Bates was now her own personal servant and groom and that her little maid Jenny thought there was nobody like him, though she flirted with him outrageously.

"We shall never come to any harm while we have Bates," she said. "Jenny and I are sure of that." She had acquired a new dignity, a new composure that discomforted him: the shyly reserved Tabbie had gone and he found himself put out by this beautiful stranger, and he was more depressed still when he learned from Blanche that there was a young baronet in Westmorland after Tabbie, and that she could not make up her mind to have him, and that was why Blanche had asked her there for Christmas.

"I did not want her to rush into another engagement that she might regret," she told her brother. "I thought if she were at the Castle for Christmas he might be there too, and it could lead to disaster. She was glad to come to West Bassett, I think. It has happy memories for her and she is fond of Sophy." She added after a moment, "I believe Lady Colleston will be in London in the spring. Tabbie is to accompany her and be introduced into society directly she is out of mourning. Her great-aunt means to present her at a Drawing-Room. Perhaps you will see her in London, Hubert."

Hubert asked his sister what made her think that he would be accustomed to mix with the society that Lady Tabitha Satterthwaite would frequent, but Blanche only laughed and told him not to be a goose, and he went home feeling that as a season of good will Christmas was sadly over-rated.

A garrulous clergyman—a Canon of the Cathedral—accompanied him as far as Ipswich, and it was not until after that that he had his first-class compartment to himself and was free to take a small photograph framed in brass out of an inner pocket and compare the girl on the breakwater with the beautiful and composed young lady of today. To that girl he had been able to say what he did about William's nightingale, but he could not say that kind of thing to Lady Tabitha. The time for that had passed.

During the following January and February his pleasant house in Wimpole Street lost a great deal of its charm, and in fact so much did it seem to confine him that he made any excuse to escape from it, until one afternoon as the spring came round again he was walking in Hyde Park when a carriage with a coat of arms on its panels stopped beside him and two ladies seated in it summoned him to them.

The silver hair of the old lady was quite eclipsed by the burnished copper of the young one, and for a moment he could only stare. Then he pulled himself together, hat in hand.

"Lady Colleston—Lady Tabitha." He made a slightly stiff bow. "I did not expect to see you in London."

"We came to buy Tabitha some dresses," Lady Colleston said. "It is great fun, is it not, Tabbie? She is so charming to dress, Dr. Ashley." Her eyes rested on the doctor pleasantly. "I hope you will call on me while I am here. We are in Cavendish Square, just round the corner from Wimpole Street. I think you know the house."

He bowed again, gave a somewhat wintry smile as he said he would be charmed, and the carriage drove on.

"Is Dr. Ashley always so cool in his manner?" Lady Colleston asked with a glance at her great niece.

"No." Cool he certainly had not been on that evening at West Bassett when they had listened to William's nightingales. But at Christmas—ah, at Christmas he had been aloof and cold and would scarcely look at her.

"Perhaps he is scared of you," her great-aunt said and added thoughtfully, "I wonder what it is like to have a physician in one's family? He could be useful: he might even cure Henry's gout."

"Nothing can cure Great-uncle Henry's gout," said Tabbie hastily, "except . . ."

"I know what you are going to say, my love, but nobody will persuade Henry to give up his port wine and his brandy and the red meat that his soul loves. But I shall speak to your Dr. Ashley about it all the same when he comes to call."

"He is not my doctor," said Tabbie quickly, but her colour was rather heightened as she spoke.

"Then he should be," said her aunt severely. "He is a very nice man, and I daresay as a doctor he will not kill you any quicker than another." She put her gloved hand on Tabbie's with an affectionate pressure. "I think he needs a little encouragement, my dear."

Tabbie did not agree. She was getting on in life, after all—twenty-five—and a man like Hubert Ashley did not want a mature woman setting her cap at him. She remembered that he had called Miss Fulgrove a man-eater and she shivered. She would make sure that she was out when he called upon her great-aunt.

The house in Cavendish Square had been freshly painted. No longer did neglect show itself in cobwebbed windows and missing area railings. Footmen were there to take him up the beautiful staircase and into her ladyship's drawing-room with the family portraits smiling down from the watered-silk walls. Hubert glanced at them to see if he could find among them Richard Satterthwaite's brilliantly blue eyes and discovered them at last in a portrait of a rather stout gentleman over the fireplace.

"You are looking at the Judge, Dr. Ashley," said Lady Colleston. "He started life as a young waster and ended up a judge before whom every criminal quailed. I daresay he knew their tricks and their manners, as Mr. Dickens makes one of his characters say in one of his charmin' novels—though I forget which one it is. The dear man writes so many, does he not? I am sorry Tabbie is not here today." But she did not seem at all put out by her niece's absence. "That nice cousin of hers—with the strange name—but no matter, we call her Sophy—called and Tabbie has taken her for a drive. She is a pleasant woman with a horde of noisy children, a great chatterer, but Tabbie is fond of her and it is good for her to see younger people. I understand that your sister married one of the Sackroyds, Dr. Ashley?"

"Yes. William Sackroyd—a good fellow."

"Sophy tells me he is the nicest of the family. I do not think I have ever met Sir Joseph or Lady Sackroyd." Her tone implied that she had no wish to meet them and her gaze rested pensively on the tall broad-shouldered gentleman who was sitting on the most uncomfortable chair in the room with his hat in his hands, listening to her as gravely as if she were describing the symptoms of some illness. "My great-niece has had a sad life, ending in a tragedy that it will take her time to get over. But she is a dear girl and I would like to see her happy."

Hubert, finding that he was expected to say something, here remarked stiffly that all Lady Tabitha's friends wanted to see her happy.

"I have brought her to London because I want to give her the balls and the dinners and parties that are hers by right," went on her ladyship serenely. "I understand that Lady Sackroyd liked to keep her in the background, and even had the impertinence to talk about the 'unfortunate' colour of her hair. It is magnificent hair. Do you not think so, Dr. Ashley?"

He was caught off his guard. "It is the most beautiful hair I have ever seen." Abruptly he pulled himself together. "But the Sackroyds, Lady Colleston, are very small beer."

"One understands that, although the Rawlings were pleased to get one of the daughters for Harry I believe, but I have never met her. I understand the dowry was in the region of thirty thousand pounds, and the poor Rawlings were always in debt. I remember years ago when I was a gal I used to visit them at Perle Place and the Rawlings' gals—Harry's great-aunts—were so ashamed of their morning dresses—they were so patched and darned. They were charmin' gals all the same and I was fond of them." She changed the subject. "Have you a garden in Wimpole Street?"

"A small back-yard."

"No room for exercise then?"

"I take my exercise riding and walking in the parks."

"Would it benefit you if I were to lend you my spare key to our gardens here in the Square? They are at the bottom of your street and you would be able to walk there any time you pleased. Friends of mine are always welcome to use them." She got up and went to a pretty toy of a secretaire in French marquetry and took a key from a drawer and gave it to him. "Tabbie takes Sophy and her children into the Square Gardens sometimes when they come to visit us. Noisy little ruffians." But she was smiling as she spoke. "You know London well I think?"

"I have lived here most of my life. At one time I was in the Army—the Foot Guards, ma'am."

"And you gave it up to become a physician?" She sounded incredulous and because she was so gentle and so kind he found himself telling her about the girl who had died at seventeen, and her sympathy was like a blessing passed on to him over the years.

Dear Tabbie, she thought, after he had gone. How excellently this nice man would suit her. She was certain that her great-niece was in love with him, by the way her colour came and went and her eyes shone when his name was mentioned, and she was as certain now that he was even more violently in love with her—did he not fire up over her hair? And the way he had told her of his past love was as if for the first time he was able to tell of it as a story that was told. But both were so prickly, so loathe to be thought to be running after the other for a variety of stupid reasons to which nobody would ever give a thought, that she would have to move with care and tact.

Well, she would give Tabbie her London season, and after an exhausting summer of balls and dinners and breakfasts they would return to Westmorland and she did not think that Tabbie would be very interested in the men who would pursue her there. She had come to her rightful place in the world too late: the years the Sackroyds had stolen could never be returned to her, and poor Tabbie, lovely as she was, was neither fish, flesh nor good red herring.

But happiness could be hers, and this Ashley man had keen and honest eyes. She felt sure that he was wise and would cherish little Tabbie and give her the happiness she had missed.

A little encouragement, Lady Colleston thought, as she shut the drawer in her pretty desk. That was all that was really needed.

She wondered if the doctor liked the opera. She thought he must as it was when he was on the way home from Covent Garden that he had seen poor Richard lying in the gutter. She would ask him to join them in their box one day next week.

CHAPTER

16

Hubert walked back to Wimpole Street with the key in his pocket, doubtful if he would ever use it. Charming as she was Lady Colleston did not understand how big was the gulf between himself and Tabbie.

For her he must always be the doctor who had told her that her father could not live, though he might remain a friend to the end of his days. He thought of the Castle in Westmorland and its magnificence, its army of servants and the head housekeeper in rustling black silk. He thought of the family, of the Earl and his wife, so kindly welcoming, so warm in their thanks for all he had done for poor Richard, and of their children, equally welcoming, equally warm in their thanks, and of *their* children, holding out shy hands gravely to take his, their small faces with the same fine bone structure as Tabbie's.

That was her world, her home, and they were her people. A physician, however fashionable, however successful, could never be accepted as a member of it, because he could not accept his position there for himself.

Maybe a certain amount of pride warred with his love for Tabbie in those days, and there were times when he regretted his move to Wimpole Street and its proximity to Cavendish Square. The Sackroyds, vulgar and purse-proud as they were, were nearer to him socially than the Satterthwaites, for all their charm.

He could not help his thoughts dwelling on Tabbie though and the look in her face when they had met in the park. Her manner might have been cool but for a moment the old Tabbie had looked at him from her eyes.

One morning on his way through the Square he heard familiar voices upraised in argument, and stopped, and on an impulse used Lady Colleston's key to let himself into the Gardens. Sophy's children were there, skipping and arguing as to how many times they could skip without stopping, while Sophy sat on an elegant bench talking animatedly to Tabbie.

Sophy saw him first. "Dr. Ashley!" she exclaimed. "Are you living in Cavendish Square too?" And then, "No, of course not. You are in Wimpole Street, but that is just a stone's throw away. Have you heard from Blanche lately? How is William? Has he found any fault with the drains again? I do hope he will not have the floor up in her pretty drawing-room." She chattered on, telling him that the children had a holiday and she had taken them to see the Panorama in Leicester Square and before going home she thought she would come and see Tabbie, and he listened gravely, not hearing a word of it.

Tabitha was out of mourning now: her Leghorn hat was trimmed with black and white ostrich feathers, and her pique dress and paletot were of the colour of golden brown leather, and were trimmed with fine tracery in a delicate black braid. A lace jabot was fastened round her throat and her face, as she raised startled eyes to his, was momentarily animated with pleasure. The May morning and the lilac that was in bloom in the Gardens was a fitting setting for one so lovely.

Sophy had suddenly realised that the children should be on their way to Camberwell and their dinners. She called the little nursemaid, now a staid sixteen, and helped her to shepherd the brood towards the gate, and Hubert took her place for a moment on the bench beside Tabbie.

"Your aunt gave me a key to these gardens," he said. "I called on her the other day, but she may not have told you."

"Yes, she told me you had called. I was sorry to have missed you." The voice was restrained and calm, the animation had left the beautiful face, and he plunged on never so much at a loss for finding conversation as now:

"I told her that I found it difficult to take enough exercise."

He was rewarded for a miraculous moment. "Oh Hubert," Tabbie said, "surely you are not afraid o' growing fat?" Her eyes laughed at him teasingly, her face was alive with mischief. "I cannot imagine you any fatter than you are."

"Am I to take that for a compliment?" he demanded "Or the reverse?"

"A compliment of course," she said. "Although I an an old enough friend to be rude to you if I please."

And then Sophy returned and chattered her way to the gate with them. Did they know that every girl baby in England was being christened Florence after Miss Night

ingale, and all the small girls were longing to grow up so
that they could become lady nurses? Hubert forgave her
for her loquaciousness, however, because as she kissed
Tabbie goodbye she said: "I shall think of you tomorrow
sitting here in this quiet square with the lilac out round
that charming little rustic bench. Do you not think Tabbie
is lucky, Dr. Ashley, to have a private garden of her own
to come to every morning?"

"She is indeed." So she came every morning: he went
his way more cheerfully than he had done in weeks, and
there were not many mornings after that when he did not
find Cavendish Square to be his quickest route to and
from his patients and the key was put to good use.

It did not take long to get back on the old happy foot-
ing with Tabbie, although there was one unhappy evening
when he was invited to the opera, and found a young
baronet from Westmorland there in Lady Colleston's box.
He rather ostentatiously turned his back on Lady Tabbie's
physician and kept her attention for himself.

But Hubert still went on using the key to the Gardens
and after a week when she did not come the young man
returned to Westmorland and Hubert found himself sitting
once more on the rustic bench under the lilacs beside
Tabbie, listening to her account of the balls she had been
to, and of the ball that was to be given for her the next
night in Cavendish Square.

"There will be the usual crush of people there," she
told him, making a little face. "My dearest aunt is
kindness itself, and when she presented me at the
Drawing-Room I did not feel nearly as frightened as I
thought I should, because she was so kind and took it for
granted that I should know how to curtsey without losing

my balance. The Queen was charming to me: she sent a message to my aunt to bring me to her afterwards. We went to the private apartments and Her Majesty spoke to me so kindly about my father, saying in her soft little voice how she had heard that he had gone out to the Crimea as a private soldier. 'He was a very brave and gallant gentleman, Lady Tabitha,' she said. 'You have every right to be proud of him, as we are of all our soldiers.' Was not that a charming thing to say?"

"Indeed yes."

"There was a time," she went on quickly, "when I felt I could never forgive my uncle and aunt for what they did to my father and to me, but looking back, as I sit here in these Gardens in the mornings, I can see now that my uncle at least treated me with kindness. It was not his fault that I was not his child and he could not care for me as if I were."

"He acted abominably and so did your aunt."

"My great-aunt says so—but I am not so sure. One does not know the contents of all those dusty cupboards where people lock up the things they do not like to remember."

He turned his head to smile at her, his eyes tender. "My dear, this is scarcely the sort of moralising for a young lady who is to have her own ball tomorrow night."

"But I have come to it all too late," she said. "It is like a ballroom one sees in a dream: you think you can catch a glimpse of the fountains playing and the brilliant colours of the dresses and the jewels of the grand company within. And then when you arrive you find the fountains have stopped, the colours have faded, the jewels are no longer there, and the grand company is all gone home."

She took the little gold watch from her waistband and seeing the time said she must go. "They are dressing me in finery that would shame a peacock tomorrow," she said as she gave him her hand. "I hope you are coming? I know my aunt sent you an invitation."

And a very grand invitation it had been, starting with the words, "The Countess of Colleston requests the pleasure of Dr. Hubert Ashley's company"—stressing the gulf that lay between his world and hers.

He had accepted it, however, and he said so, and although he did not add that he did not intend to be there, there was something in his face that made her doubt him and she said, suddenly vexed with him, "I shall not forgive you if you do not come. I am depending upon you—as I depend on all my old friends." And then as he stood silent, with a touch of impatience, "Have you forgotten that you danced the first dance with me at Louisa's wedding?"

How could he forget? "But there will be many others waiting to claim that privilege tomorrow night," he reminded her.

"Oh," she said, the glint of tears in her eyes, "why are you so grave and stern with me? May we not be friends, as we were before?"

"No."

"But why?" She was hurt by his abrupt unkindness.

"Because I am in love with you," he said quietly. "Because I have been in love with you ever since that February night last year when it was drizzling with rain and you put your hand in mine, as you did just now. That is why I shall not come to your ball, Tabbie, and I shall not ask you to dance with me again. I would give my life for you gladly—but there are some things I cannot do and there are some things you must not ask me to do." And then he left her, striding across the Gardens to Wimpole Street.

He arrived late at the ball on the following night. The awning was stretched above the red carpet from the top of the steps to the pavement and across it, and all night the carriages arrived as the great ones of the land alighted and made their way up the staircase to the state rooms above. The ballroom was vast and scented with banks of flowers, the bands were muted, the dancing, unlike the Sackroyds' romps, as decorous as it should be, even to the waltz.

Hubert caught sight of Tabbie in the distance in a dress of shimmering green gauze that made her look lovelier than he remembered ever having seen her before. She had emeralds round her neck and in her hair and there was a posy of white camelias in her hand.

He stood for a while against the wall watching her, and the Satterthwaites sought him out and were very kind to him, and found partners for him: charming young ladies who were a little bit puzzled at first when he told them he was a physician and then found his place in the household for him by saying that of course he was the friend who had been so kind to Tabbie's poor dear papa.

Directly he could he slipped away, turning his back on the red carpet and the awning and the muted bands, and walked back to Wimpole Street and sat there for a long time in his study, staring at a little brass framed seaside photograph, until the day was dawning and the carriages were beginning to depart at the bottom of the road.

Then because he might shock Mrs. Webb if she were to find him still in his evening clothes at his desk at that hour of the morning, he went to his room and got undressed and went to bed, but he was still awake when his man came to call him.

At about noon that day a carriage stopped outside his door and he was told that a lady wished to see him. Thinking that it was a professional call he told the servant to show her in, and she came in and stood there smiling at him.

"I have come to scold you," she said. "You did not ask me to dance and you left before supper, when my health was drunk. I missed you and I think it was unkind of you."

He stood very still by his writing-table. "I told you why I could not ask you to dance," he said.

She came over to him and stood there, examining his cravat with her head on one side. "You are not like William," she said. "I cannot put your hair straight because there is never a hair out of place. You are meticulously correct, although now I come to think of it it does look the merest bit rumpled this morning. And your man was not thinking what he was doing when he tied your cravat today. I can at least put that straight." She raised her hands to his cravat, and found them seized in a grip that hurt.

"Tabbie, you little wretch," Hubert said. "What are you doing to me? How can you marry me, now that you have found your own world?"

"It isn't my world," she said gently. "It is theirs—the Satterthwaites'. My world is here, with you—if you will have me, Hubert."

His arms came round her roughly, pulling her close, and he bent his head and kissed her, long and deep, and when he released her he said hoarsely, "Did Jarrett ever kiss you like that?"

"Never," she said. She was flushed and her eyes were shining: she was her father's daughter. "Oh, Hubert, my darling—kiss me again!"

Another Georgette Heyer Novel
from Fawcett Crest—

THE MASQUERADERS   Crest Q2692 $1.50

This joyous romp of a novel is a delightful tangle of adventure and romance that will keep you entranced from first page to last.

Temporarily abandoned by their scapegrace father, Prudence and Robin Lacey are forced to masquerade as the opposite sex to avoid capture by their political enemies.

Prue makes a devilishly handsome young man and her brother Robin is equally beguiling as her "sister."

This, however, makes for some dangerous entanglements when Prue, as Mr. Merriot, falls in love with Sir Anthony, and her brother, posing as Miss Merriot, finds his heart struck by the lovely heiress, Letty Grayson. . . .

Georgette Heyer has never created more spirited or amusing characters nor spun a livelier web of intrigue and derring-do.

"Reading Georgette Heyer is the next best thing to reading Jane Austen."

—*Publishers Weekly*

FAWCETT CREST BESTSELLERS